M000231189

DEATHBED
Confessions

Criminal Sends Plea to Former Lawman

A novel by

SHERIFF GERALD HEGE

This is a work of fiction. All of the characters, names, incidents,
organizations, and dialogue in this novel are either the products
of the author's imagination or are used fictitiously.

LifeRich Publishing is a registered trademark of
The Reader's Digest Association, Inc.

LifeRich Publishing books may be ordered through booksellers or by contacting:

LifeRich Publishing
1663 Liberty Drive
Bloomington, IN 47403
www.liferichpublishing.com
1 (888) 238-8637

Because of the dynamic nature of the Internet, any web addresses or
links contained in this book may have changed since publication and
may no longer be valid. The views expressed in this work are solely those
of the author and do not necessarily reflect the views of the publisher,
and the publisher hereby disclaims any responsibility for them.

Any people depicted in stock imagery provided by Thinkstock are models,
and such images are being used for illustrative purposes only.
Certain stock imagery © Thinkstock.

ISBN: 978-1-4897-1168-7 (sc)
ISBN: 978-1-4897-1167-0 (e)

Library of Congress Control Number: 2017904034

Print information available on the last page.

LifeRich Publishing rev. date: 03/16/2017

To my mom, Vivian, who loved to read crime stories.

Many thanks to Bob Burchette, Etta Moseley, and Geri Hege for their assistance in the production of my first novel. I appreciate all they have done.

Contents

Dying Criminal Wants to See Ex-Lawman

"Blueberry Hill wants to be friends on Facebook"

When I saw that friend request on Facebook, it struck me as a strange profile name and I ignored it for a couple of days. I receive dozens of friend requests every week and in most cases, I don't know the person making the request. If they already have a lot of my friends on their profile, I may do a little research and then confirm the friend request.

However, Blueberry Hill did remind me of a song by one of my favorite recording artists, Fats Domino. I found myself singing:

> *I found my thrill on Blueberry Hill*
> *On Blueberry Hill when I found you.*
>
> *The moon stood still on Blueberry Hill*
> *And lingered until my dream came true.*

My mom had also loved the song and I think it was for this reason I finally confirmed the Facebook request. In less than an hour, I heard from Blueberry Hill:

Dear Sheriff,

I know you probably are wondering about this profile name, but let me first thank you for accepting my friend request. I am writing on behalf of my father who has cancer and has only a few weeks to live. He desperately wants to see you. He was in your jail back in 2001 and also appeared on your TV show. He really enjoyed that show you had on the Court TV Network. He had never seen a reality show where prisoners discussed their crimes with the sheriff. You may remember that my dad was a lifelong criminal. Sheriff, you left quite an impression on him and he told me you even helped find him a job when he got out of jail. He was the one who worked on antique cars. He told me that you and he once rode around the county in your Spider car and you asked him questions about how you determined which houses to break into. While you were riding around, you had a Fats Domino CD playing and when Fats sang "Blueberry Hill," you and dad started singing along.

Dad liked that song so much that he made it his alias after he got out of your jail, but he usually just goes by BH. That's why I'm using Blueberry Hill on Facebook.

Dad told me that you are known as a tough guy and it surprised him when you showed your human side. Over the years, he has told people about that ride and being on your show and how you didn't believe some of his tales. I am sorry if I am taking up your time but I know of no other way to get you to remember him. He said after the day you rode him around, you would call him Blueberry Hill every time you saw him.

A few years after dad left North Carolina, he bought an old plantation down here in Louisiana. The place is a few miles from the little farm my husband Sam and I own.

I hadn't seen him in 15 years and I was shocked when he showed up my door. Dad was pretty drunk and said that he finally had gotten up nerve enough to come see me. He knew where I lived and had been putting off coming over here. He apologized several times for not being a father to me for all of these years. He stayed with us for several days and told us all kinds of stories. One of his tales was that he had the winning lottery ticket in the old truck he was driving.

We didn't pay any attention to what he said about that ticket. Our concern was for getting him sober. He wasn't out of the way or anything; in fact, he was rather humble.

After he kept insisting he had the winning ticket in his old truck, my husband went out and got a stack of papers from the truck. Sure enough, stuck to a candy wrapper was a lottery ticket.

Dad insisted that I call and check on that number before he left. He said he had to get back to his farm because his friends would be worried about him. He hadn't told them that he even had a daughter, and they surely didn't know that I was living within a few miles of them.

I called to check on the lottery ticket as dad sat at the kitchen table. After reading the numbers to the lady on the phone, I sat down. In about thirty seconds, the lady came back on and said, "Congratulations, you have a winning number for 2.7 million dollars."

I nearly passed out. Needless to say, the ticket changed our lives. Dad was afraid to claim the ticket because of his criminal record. He was afraid that because he is a felon, the ticket might be voided.

He had us to collect on the ticket and told me to handle the money. He said he was going to use some of the money to buy the old plantation down the road from us and we could keep the rest. I couldn't believe it! He said he had plenty of money but it was hidden away and he didn't want to touch it.

Dad was feeling much better when he left. He told us not to come over to the farm where he was living until he got back in touch with us. "The people I live with are sort of funny and don't like anybody much to come around. I'll be back in touch and we will spend some time together," he said.

"I didn't hear from him for several months. Then this big guy who said his name was Ralph came to our farm and told us that dad wanted see us down at the old plantation. It was the place that he bought with his lottery winnings.

Sam and I followed Ralph back down there.

Ralph showed us to a bedroom where my dad was lying down. He looked pale and sort of depressed when we walked in. But he smiled when he saw us.

He hugged my neck as best he could without getting out of bed. Dad wanted to talk to us. The news was bad, he said. He had only a few weeks to live; he had been diagnosed with cancer.

I began to sob. But he told me not to do that; he didn't like crying. What was on his mind was all of the horrible things he had done. He didn't want to die without telling someone about them. It sounded like he wanted to make a confession. I suggested that he tell me or I would get a priest to come by to hear his confession. He didn't want that.

There was only one person he wanted to hear what he had to say. I asked him who he wanted to hear his confession. He said, "Sheriff Crawford up in North Carolina. See if you can get him to come down here and listen to what I want to say before I die."

Sheriff, he really wants to confess – I guess you can call it that. He wants to tell you about the awful things he has done. If you could find it in your heart, we will gladly pay you and all your expenses to get here. He is sitting over there in that big house and asks me every day if I have heard from you. He said, "I know he will come if you can get a hold of him I know he will."

Chapter One

Old Crook Remembered

Deathbed confessions aren't new to me. But I must say the request from Blueberry Hill's daughter comprised the longest message I've ever received on Facebook.

I knew right away who this old crook using the name Blueberry Hill was; he was the most interesting prisoner I had ever had in my jail. Seeing him again might be exciting.

Hearing his deathbed confession would be a rare opportunity to look closer at the mind of one of the most unique criminals I had known.

He was using some other bogus name when he was arrested in Davidson County, NC. Of the thousands of criminals I dealt with during my career, he was, without a doubt, the most fascinating one. The crimes he told me about were so bizarre and so awful I just knew he was lying. Yet, I had been able to confirm every terrible story he had told. He couldn't be charged with any of those crimes now because the statute of limitations had expired, but true they were. Of course, I don't know about other crimes he may have committed that he hadn't shared or things he had done after he left my jail.

It was also bizarre that he was using Blueberry Hill as his name. I remembered his nice baritone voice and despite his having little education, his speech had been close to perfect. He could easily have been a radio announcer. He also had an older John Wayne look about him... good looking but in a rough wind-burned way.

He stood about six feet two inches tall with brownish blonde hair. His arms and neck were covered with tattoos of dragons and snakes. I figured he must have served in the Navy. His arms and neck also had tattoos: an anchor and the name of a battleship. By the looks of them, all of the tattoos were done professionally except the several on his hands. Those had all the traits of having been done in prison. The teardrop tattoo just below his left eye, which is supposed to signify he had killed someone, had definitely been put on by a prison buddy.

I had been planning a trip to Denver, Colorado, anyway, and figured I could swing down from North Carolina to Louisiana and spend a few hours or even a couple days listening to what Blueberry Hill had to say.

I know the area where he was living because I had been stationed in that area at Fort Polk, LA., while in the Army. Before I was sent to Vietnam, I got to know my way around the little river towns on the Bayou.

It would be a twelve or thirteen-hour drive down to the land of many bridges and swamps. This would give me time to think more about crimes the man told me he had committed. I felt sure he hadn't told me about all of his crimes. "This could really be interesting," I said to myself.

I had no way of knowing the adventure I was about to embark on would be the darkest and most intriguing experience of my life.

Blueberry Hill's daughter sent directions to the old plantation where her father was living. For the trip, I chose my dad's old 1994 Chevrolet Geo which has three cylinders and gets forty-eight miles per gallon. It's not much to look at but I love to drive it. I put a couple of shirts and camouflaged pants into a trash bag and headed south down I-85. I've made the trip to Atlanta and New Orleans a dozen times so there was no need for a map.

Since I was a young boy, I have loved to drive and couldn't wait to get behind the wheel of the little blue Geo. I am always amazed at my friends who love to ask me about my latest travels. Most of these friends are about my age, 67. You would think they are all around 100 years old because they fret about driving on long trips.

All of them have better vehicles than I have, and they damn sure have more money. You would have thought I was going to the moon by the reactions I got from them when I said I was going to be driving twelve hours or more by myself. My friends mostly go nowhere.

Most of these friends take daily "trips" to town every morning to eat breakfast, then make about five trips during the day to my parents' old store on Ridge Road near Pilgrim, NC. Hanging around the store is a favorite pastime for my friends. They usually drink a Coke and tell a few lies and leave. They drift back in and out of the store during the day and have another Coke and engage in more conversations before it's time to go home.

My friends on Facebook are the same way. They say they would like to travel but never do. They would love to see all the places I have been, but have a thousand reasons why they don't take a good trip. I tell them how surprised they would be at the small cost of a road trip in America.

It's funny how many women take to traveling as soon as their husbands die. One of my neighbors, who has since passed, told me a story about how tight her husband was. She said, "I'm going to make him turn over in his grave. I going to wipe all the dust off that money and enjoy the rest of my life." She spent the next several years doing just that.

My trip to Bayou country to meet Blueberry Hill was uneventful until I found a crab and oyster shack near the river. One of the first things I do on the Bayou is find one of those shacks. I like the dirty shacks with the moss hanging down and plenty of dirty pickup

3

trucks in the parking lot. These are just regular folks who make their living from the rivers and bayous of Louisiana. After twelve hours of driving, I knew I wanted at least a dozen raw oysters. I can easily eat three dozen but I would settle for a small meal.

An older white woman with a few teeth missing and a big smile placed melted butter and crackers and a cold beer in front of me. She was wearing a white apron with ketchup and mustard stains from top to bottom. A bright yellow ribbon tied in a bow on top of her head accented her long gray hair. As she popped the top off the brew, she said, "What brings y'all down to the bayou?" Her distinct Cajun drawl sounded like someone trying to talk with peanuts in his mouth.

Just above me was an old ceiling fan, and near it was a sign in bright red letters: "If you don't like the service, just leave."

Soon I was engaged in conversation with several locals. In less than thirty minutes, I had offers to go fishing, shrimping and, of course, to drink some of the local moonshine. A couple of my new acquaintances said I looked like that sheriff who used to have a TV show. I told them I had heard that a lot but it was probably the gray hair that was confusing them.

Stopping at the little shack put me in the Louisiana mood and that would prepare me for my meeting with BH. It also helped me to remember more about him. He had started breaking into homes when he was just a little boy. His dad was a drunk and a thief who would take him into the larger cities to deliver oysters and shrimp to restaurants and pubs. While there his dad had him stealing radios from cars and his dad sold to pawnshops for five dollars each. He quickly graduated to robbing drunks in the alleys behind the bars.

One of his uncles taught him the art of cracking small safes, which were stolen from backrooms of businesses where gambling was rampant. Owners wouldn't call the police so there were no worries about getting caught, he said. He did get shot at a couple times, he told me.

He bought a small pistol with the money given to him by his

father. Then he moved on up to robbing people he would follow to their vehicles when they left the clubs. Most of his victims didn't report the crimes because they didn't want their wives to discover they had been to a bar or a brothel. According to him, he made a good living being a thug.

BH left school after the seventh grade and started driving his own car at the ripe old age of fifteen. By the time he was sixteen, he had two friends working under him. Another uncle had an auto body repair shop out in the country. He moved into a room in the back of the shop and began to learn the trade of rebuilding antique cars. This provided a perfect cover for his crime sprees and to some, it provided an appearance that he was a good young man who was trying to be successful.

He told me he had no intentions of being a good person. He loved the power that came along with being a criminal. The feeling of having complete control of another human being was like being able to have sex with several women at the same time, he said. "You know it will never happen but once, but you will always have the dream in your head."

The man who would come to be known simply as BH, told me he became obsessed with sex. That led him to start picking up older women at bars and taking them to motels and engaging in kinky sex. That added to his obsession with power and control. When intimidation and fear didn't get women to do kinky things, he raped them. Now he had become a complete psychopath. He knew it would be only a matter of time until he killed someone.

As I was leaving the oyster shack, an old man yelled, "What do you do for a living, fellow?" I walked back over to the table and said," I'm just an old man waiting at the stoplight of life." He held up his beer and said, "Hell, I'll drink to that."

I love driving the roads around the Bayou. With every curve, there is another old shack or house facing the water. Old rusted cars are scattered around the yards of many of these homes. Unfinished fishing boats sitting on sawbucks in need of repair are common sites.

Most of the old boats will never be repaired. It's like the people use their junk as a badge of honor as if to tell passing motorists, "We don't have much but it's paid for."

About three miles from my destination, I pulled into a country store to get a little gasoline. It had once been an old Sinclair station like the ones we used to have throughout Davidson County years ago. I didn't know there were any more around.

Before I could roll out of the Geo, an elderly man came out of the store wearing bib overalls and a baseball cap. "Fill her up, young man?" he asked.

"Go ahead but be careful. It only holds ten gallons," I said. He laughed and said, "Sure thing"

When I went inside to pay for the gas, I noticed a display of hand-rolled cigars behind the counter. The cigars were made in New Orleans at a place called the Cigar Factory. I figured the cigars were a bargain at only $2 each, and I bought a handful. At the Factory they cost $7. I am not a big smoker but there is something special about a cigar. It's a feeling of freedom to roll one around in your mouth; that must be a man thing. I can't inhale the cigars but I like the feeling it gives me as I'm driving down the road or talking with a killer in a dark room.

Finally, I came to a landmark, which had been given to me by BH's daughter. It was an Old Dutch style barn located at the intersection of Frog Foot Road and Big Bass Gulch Road. The directions were to go down one mile on Frog Foot and look for two big river rock columns with a rusty gate. I found the gate and slowly pulled the Geo into the driveway. The drive was lined with giant magnolia trees. They were spread about fifty yards apart. We'd had a big one in our front yard when I was a kid, but it didn't compare with the size of these trees.

Though rusted, the large gate showed signs of once having been an expensive investment for someone. The opening must have been over thirty feet wide and at least twelve feet high. If you were to install a gate like this now, it would cost at least twenty-thousand dollars. In the center of the gate, was a large crest, a single carriage being pulled by large horse. On each side of the crest were the magnolias. The crest was done in brass, which had turned green from years of being battered by the weather.

I had been told BH didn't have a phone but his daughter would tell him when to expect me at his house. Her father would be sitting on the front porch, she said.

The sand graveled road created a unique sound as the small pebbles were thrown underneath the Geo. I drove slowly so I could enjoy the smell of the large white flowers of the magnolias. I've always figured the smell is a cross between the sweet honeysuckle and pumpkin pulp.

The driveway was over a mile long with no houses in site. I reached a small driveway to the right and made a turn. That driveway also was lined with magnolias. It was another two-hundred yards to the house. The two-story house was straight out of *Gone with the Wind*. I kept looking for a sign, which read "Tara," the fictional plantation in the movie. The driveway made a circle around an old fountain with a bronze statue of a Civil War soldier in the center. It was obvious the fountain hadn't functioned in decades.

All the grounds and gardens had fallen to neglect and disrepair many years ago. Sure enough, sitting in a wheelchair on the porch was a frail and dark figure of a man. On the broken red tile floor of the porch was a green oxygen tank. A long clear plastic tube wound from the tank to his nose. Between his legs was a homemade cane. My dad had owned several similar canes and usually gave the impression that although he was in a wheel chair, he could probably walk a short distance with the cane.

Peering through the windshield at the figure on the porch, I couldn't find a single feature that reminded me of the man I had known years ago. I glanced in my rear view mirror and thought, "You don't look familiar, either." I opened the door and got out like I was an old man, too. The little Geo is pretty low to the ground, and trying to get a six-foot four-inch frame out of it is a challenge.

As soon as I straightened myself out, the man on the porch yelled, "Hello, Sheriff, how the hell are you?" He was wearing a red and black-checkered bathrobe and stood up with the aid of his cane.

"Keep your seat," I said, heading toward the red brick steps.

He stretched towards me and shook my hand with a weak squeeze.

"Have a seat," he said, pointing towards an old Kennedy rocker. I knew it was a Kennedy rocker because they once were made in North Carolina. I'd had one but my wife had given it away. To answer his earlier question, I told him I was doing fine for an old man who had been driving all day in a cracker box. He laughed and said, "I had one of those things years ago. Stole it in Texas. Small but damn good on gas."

BH still had that charisma and big smile. His white hair was in a ponytail. His big robin egg eyes were surveying me up and down. "Sheriff, you haven't changed a lot, maybe put on a few pounds." He also had good eyesight.

We chatted on the porch for a few minutes before going inside the house. The ceilings in the house were about 15 feet high and from the period of the old plantation. A great room loomed up at the end of the wide hallway. I could see water spots on the ceiling and faded brown rings around them. Surprisingly, the interior of the home was neat and clean. I could smell the mildew but most old homes have that odor. Six-inch crown molding used in the construction of the house gave it a feeling of having once been a place of wealth and success.

I could imagine grand parties being held here with everyone arriving in their horse drawn carriages. The men would be wearing top hats, and the ladies would be flaunting big dresses and lots of hair. More likely they were arriving in 1936 Ford coupes or big black Lincolns.

We made our way to the great room with mahogany walls lined with old photos of several old people. A huge fireplace was located at the end of the room. I guessed the room was forty feet by thirty feet. Placed around the room were several red velvet chairs and a large couch to match. I remember this type of furniture being used by my neighbor, Mrs. Ethel Morgan. I had thought it was great to sit on the velvet at Mrs. Morgan's and look at the black lines woven into the cloth.

No doubt, this was at one time one fancy and regal place. It would take over a million dollars to replace something like this place today.

BH, moving with his cane in hand, told me to follow him to the back porch. "I think you will like it out here," he said, as he opened the large French doors. Another large broken red tile porch overlooking a large lake awaited us. Wicker chairs provided us seats.

As I was sitting down, BH yelled, "Ralph, bring me and the sheriff a drink and one of those cigars." I looked at him and asked about Ralph. I was told BH lived alone. He told me that Ralph was a friend of his. They had spent five years together in a state prison for armed robbery and assault.

In a few minutes, a large elderly white man appeared in the doorway. In his hand was a tray containing a bottle of Jack Daniels and two huge Cuban cigars. The man appeared to be older than both of us but looked to be in excellent physical shape. I could tell he had once worked out on a regular basis. I took the cigar and a small glass of Jack and after I licked the cigar a few times, Ralph produced a large lighter and fired it up. "Nice to meet you, Sheriff Crawford. I have read a lot about you and BH has a lot of respect for you; that makes you okay with me," Ralph said.

I love to meet people like Ralph, although I didn't have any idea about his real character. I could sense the friendship between the two men. It was amazing that the two of them who had once lived in a six-foot by six-foot prison cell for five years were now sitting on the back porch of an old mansion smoking Cuban cigars and drinking Jack.

We spent about an hour smoking the cigars and listening to BH and Ralph talk about the old days. Ralph was finally dismissed and I knew it was time to get down to the reason I had come to see BH.

"Tell me how I can help you," I said. "Your daughter said something about making a confession. What's that about?" I said.

"That's right, Sheriff. I want to get all of this off my chest before I die. And you are the best person I know to understand it. My daughter told me she has explained my condition. The doctors told me there is nothing else they can do for me. But first I want to thank you for taking the time to drive all the way down here to hear my story," he said as he slid his chair closer to the wicker table. He took a sip of the Jack and began his story.

Call it a confession if you will but in my wildest imagination, I could not figure out what I was about to hear. I had heard some of his stories years earlier in my jail in Pilgrim, NC, but those tales were merely a warm-up to what I was about to hear.

"Sheriff, I know you are aware of some of the really bad things in my past. I have spent much of my life behind bars but I don't hold any grudges against anyone for that. What I did, I did with full knowledge that what I was doing was wrong. As you know, many people in prison read the Bible, and most of us can quote it better than a Baptist preacher on a Wednesday night in the middle of August.

Chapter Two

Haunted by Victims' Faces

"I have read the Good Book cover to cover over fifty times," BH said. "Throughout the years, I mostly took it to be stories simply passed down from generation to generation. I figured each teller added their own version of the facts. It's no different than the fisherman who caught the big fish. When he caught it, it was twelve inches long. By the time he finished the story at the pub, it was twenty-four inches.

"Sheriff, I don't claim to be a Christian or know if I am right or wrong about those stories in the Bible. I never saw anything God did for me. He gave me a father who beat me and taught me how to steal and hurt other people. I never knew any true love or affection by anyone. My mom ran off with a drug dealer when I was five years old.

"For a period of seven years, I took my hatred out on a lot of people. I wanted them to experience the hurt and pain I had to endure. Even though they were all strangers, I wanted them to suffer and in my mind, I wanted them to be sent to Heaven or hell in a horrible way. What I am about to tell you is all the truth. I know I will burn in hell for eternity, as I should, if there really is such a place."

BH was silent for a moment; his head was drooped as if he were thinking about what the future held for him. By the look on his face, I figured he was at peace with his thoughts and had no reason to hold anything back.

"Are you sure you want to divulge this information?" I asked.

"I have to get it off my mind," he blurted. "All I can see at night are the faces of my victims. I haven't slept in a month. I have to get it off my mind."

Then he got into his story which I soon discovered was only the first of many confessions.

"I finished repairing and painting an old pickup truck for a man who owned a bar outside New Orleans," BH said. "It was getting dark so I decided I would deliver the truck the next day. My uncle had other ideas and told me the owner wanted it delivered that night. I took the hour to drive to town and found the owner behind the bar in the alley. I gave him the keys and the bill. My uncle was going to pick me up, but it would be at least two hours before he arrived. The owner of the car told me to come inside and have a few drinks.

"The bar began to fill up with customers, and a cover band started playing some old songs by Hank Williams. I noticed a small table over near the Jukebox. Sitting at the table was a white lady who appeared to be in her thirties. She was wearing a blue dress with a small white collar. A large white man joined her in a few minutes. They soon were laughing and drinking. Both were smoking and as I watched the smoke surround her face, it brought back memories of my mother.

"My mother would take me to the home of one of her many boyfriends after Dad had passed out. She made me stay on the front porch or in the living room while she sat in the kitchen drinking and smoking. At one house, there was a mirror on the wall and I could see into the kitchen. Her friend was all over her. He was kissing her and grabbing her. He pulled her hair and gave her drinks out of a brown bottle. I wanted to kill him.

"Eventually, they went into a back room. When she came out, I saw the man give her money. She gave me a dollar. 'Now honey, there is no need for your daddy to know about our visit.'

"My mother was wearing a blue dress with a white collar."

"After about thirty minutes, the man with the woman in the bar got up from the table and left the building, BH said. "In less than two minutes, the lady came over to my table. 'Well, aren't you a cutie; all alone are you?' I told her I was alone and after a couple of drinks, she asked me if I would like to take a ride and maybe go to another bar. I knew I had to be back so I could ride back with my uncle. I also knew he wouldn't care where I was as long as the man gave him his money for the work on the car.

"We left the bar and started walking down the street. I asked her what she was driving and she told me she didn't have a car. She put her arm around my waist and said, 'We can walk to where we are going, Sweetie.' We walked a couple of blocks and approached an old empty building on the right. It was once a shoe shop. The faded image of an old shoe logo could still be seen on the side.

"She stopped in front of the building to light a cigarette. Then she started kissing me on my cheeks and then on my mouth. I just snapped. With images of my mother in my head, I pushed her inside of the building and began to slap her in the face. I knocked her down to her knees and put my hand on her mouth. She started coughing. I believe she swallowed the cigarette. I pulled off my belt and put it around her neck and started chocking her. I sat on her and choked her until she passed out.

"I could see her eyes shining from light from a nearby street light coming through the window. I just looked at her. I felt good. I told myself she probably had kids at home and cared only about herself. She deserved it. I waited for nearly thirty minutes just to make sure she was dead. She was dead but this was not enough. I wanted to punish her more but it would take me a while to decide what I wanted to do.

"There was an old mattress on the floor of the building. I placed it over her and left. I went back to the pub and my uncle was waiting on me. We left and all the way back home, I started planning what I was going to do.

"I knew I had to go back and get the body and take it out in the country. I knew exactly where I would take the body and what I was going to do with it."

"When my uncle dropped me off at the shop, I waited for him to drive out of sight before I got the tow truck and hooked up to an old van, which was sitting in the back of the shop. I drove down to the abandoned house where I had left the woman's body. I parked in front of the house and cut on the flashers of the tow truck. If anyone passed by, they would think I was just towing a vehicle. The hour was late but I knew I had to take care of the body under the cover of darkness.

"I took the body out and put it in the van and quickly closed the side door.

"Driving back toward my uncle's shop, I met a deputy sheriff. He waved as we passed and I didn't figure he was suspicious seeing me out that late. He probably knew we towed a lot of vehicles for the sheriff's department and it wasn't unusual to see me out at all times, day or night.

"About a half mile on the back side of my uncle's property was an old farm house. Nobody had lived there for several years but my uncle kept the electricity on. He did that so he wouldn't have to get the building inspector out there again, and risk the inspector's finding an inspections violation at the old place.

"After going to the back lot and cranking up the four-wheeler, I went inside and grabbed my electric saw and put in a fine blade. I got the woman's body out of the van and strapped it to the front rack.

"I pulled around to a small block building behind the house. It was once used to kill hogs and cut up meat. I pulled close to the large sliding doors, opened them, and placed the body on the large table. Then I took her clothes off but I left her shoes on. I don't really know why but it turned me on.

"It took about forty- five minutes for me to cut-up the body. The head came off first then both arms. The concrete floor had a large drain and I left the water running from a nearby faucet. I next cut the legs in half at the knees. The last things I cut off were the feet. I left the shoes on them. I had helped my uncle kill a lot of hogs when I was a boy so I knew how to cut up the body and package it.

"I drove back to the shop and got paper that we used to tape out the cars with. I also got some reinforced packaging tape. We used it to package car parts.

"I returned to the farm and wrapped the body parts in the paper. The packages were real neat and clean. I washed down the floor with the water hose. I know it sounds crazy to you, Sheriff, but all of this was very exciting.

"I really don't know why I went to so much trouble but it just came to me. My first thought was to take the body parts down to a county dumpster and throw it in. Suddenly, I remembered my uncle was filling in a big gulley about two hundred yards from the main garage. He allowed people to get rid of their dirt by dumping it into the gulley; he leveled out the fill dirt with the Bobcat. His intention was to build another paint shop on that spot once he got the gully filled in.

"I tied the packages to the ATV and drove them to the gulley. The gulley was about fifteen feet deep and forty yards long. There were about ten piles of dirt waiting to be pushed into the hole. It took about two hours of pushing dirt with the Bobcat for me to get the body packages covered and the dirt spread in a way I knew my uncle would want it.

"I pulled the ATV into the wash shop and I cleaned and dried it down. I waited about an hour and then drove it up and down the dirt road several times. That put a good coat of dust on it.

"I took the van back to the spot where I had hooked to it hours earlier. By this time, I was ready to get some sleep before everyone came into work."

Blueberry Hill's confession was interesting but it was disgusting, too; I was getting tired of listening to all of the details. I needed a break.

I stood up at the table and told BH I needed to stretch. Then I took a break by walking down to the lake. Looking over the lake, which probably was about five acres, I pulled out another cigar. Bending down on one knee, I lit it and thought, "This is one cold-blooded crazy individual." He reminded me of a guy I had served with in Vietnam. He did three tours over there and had to be forced to come home. He loved to kill, and it didn't matter to him who he killed.

Looking back across the lake toward the house, I saw BH sitting there with a cigar in his hand with the oxygen tank at his side. I told myself it would better if I just walked back up there and cut his throat and let him bleed to death on the porch.

However, I knew I wanted to hear the rest of his story if for no other reason than to fulfill my promise to his daughter.

As I walked across the dam of the lake, a beautiful Irish setter joined me. His coat was wavy and shiny. I bent over and gave him a rub on the head and he followed me back to the house. BH said, "I see you met George; he is my buddy."

George sat down beside BH as if he were going to listen to his master's story, as well. BH took a puff off the stogie and continued his story.

"Around 7 a.m., my uncle came to work and it was just another workday for me. I figured I should stay around, and not leave the shop for a while. If it were discovered that the woman was missing, people might think something was up if I left town.

"A week went by and I didn't hear anything about a missing woman; and my uncle continued moving dirt into the hole. I felt pretty good about everything. I really was not worried about it at all. A month went by and still nothing came up about my victim.

"My uncle asked if I would like to make a trip up to New York. He had a friend up there who had found a good deal on some dealer trade-ins. Storage space was limited in the city which forced the car dealerships to sell off trade-ins in bulk. They would give you a price on a row which might have ten or fifteen cars in the row.

"I jumped at the chance to go. My uncle had a nice seven-car hauler with a sleeper and I had never been to the Big Apple.

"Two days later, I was on the road and we arrived around midnight. A big parking lot across from the dealership was a good place for me to park the truck.

"I bedded down for the night in the sleeper. The next morning, I met the man at the dealership and was told my uncle already had picked out the row of cars he wanted. All I needed to do was to pick up the cars the following day when the paper work for the purchase would be finished.

"The dealership guy told me there was a shower in the back of the dealership where I could clean up. After taking a shower, I went back to the truck and slept until dark.

"Early in the evening, I tumbled out of the truck sleeper and decided I wanted to find some entertainment. Folks I talked to on the street told me about a nearby club that had a really good band and served great burgers. I headed that way.

"I found a bar before I got to the club. I hung around the bar until about nine o'clock that night, then went over to The Walk Away lounge.

"Sure enough, the band was good and the burger was even better. Just before midnight, a young blond haired girl came in alone, wearing tight-fitting jeans and a white blouse. There were probably around fifty people in the bar. I was sitting at a small table near the door to the ladies restroom. I picked that table on purpose so I could get a close look at the girls as they waited in line to use the restroom. The blond got in line and then lit a cigarette. The way she was putting the cigarette to her lips gave me a rush and I knew then I had to get with her.

"After about five minutes of waiting, she asked if she could sit down in the only other chair at my table.

"Sure," I said, feeling like my plan to attract a girl was working.

"We made small talk for a few minutes, and she asked me to order her a rum and Coke as she went into the restroom. In a few minutes, she returned and took a seat. We had several drinks, and she told me her life story. She was hooked on cocaine and wanted to know if I would buy her a bag. The woman didn't have any money but would trade it out for sex.

"I told her I would think about it. I didn't tell her anything about myself. She made her way around the room. I finished my drink while she worked every table trying to score a bag of the white stuff.

"I watched her pathetic behavior, begging for money and dope. I knew then what I wanted to do.

"About twenty minutes later she was back at my table. She was sweating like a lifeguard on a hot day at the beach. I told her I had a truck with a sleeper which was parked nearby. We walked to the truck as she continued to tell me about her life. She said that she left home in Ohio and worked tables with the hopes getting a job as a paralegal in New York. She had a business degree and came from a good family. She got hooked on dope while in college.

"I opened the truck door and we climbed in. I cranked up the truck. Without saying a word she immediately climbed into the sleeper and started taking off her clothes. The sight of this just made me go crazy! I jumped into the sleeper and grabbed her by the shoulders and asked her what she was doing. Before she said anything I began beating her in the face with my fists. Her nose began bleeding and she started slapping at me. I got her in a headlock and choked her down. Just as I did the woman before, I used my belt to finish her.

"I pushed her body to one side of the sleeper, and I slept beside her until the next morning. Around eight a.m. I saw the manager of the dealership arrive at work. He told me to pull the truck to the used car lot and he would have someone assist me with loading the cars.

"I went back to the truck and pulled the sleeper curtain shut, then drove over to the used car lot. About an hour later, the truck was loaded and I was ready to head south to the shop. In another couple hours, I pulled into a rest area along I-95 and opened the curtain to take a look at the woman. I put my hand on her stomach and she was already stiff. I looked around for a spot to put the body but there was too much traffic. I decided to wait until it was late and dark out.

"When I reached the Mississippi state line, it was around midnight. I pulled into a parking area where I was able to get the last parking spot down near a lake. I got out of the truck and stretched my legs as I walked down to an area below my parking space. The area appeared once to have been a picnic shelter. The shelter was gone but the concrete slab was still there. Below the slab was a large drainage pipe which I figured was nearly three feet in diameter.

"I made sure no one was around and I used the truck to hide the view. I carried the woman's body down to the big pipe and pushed it as far back into the pipe as I could reach. Then I held onto the edge of the pipe and used my legs to shove the body farther into the pipe.

"I checked the inside of my truck and left. Ten miles down the road, I pulled over and threw her purse down an embankment. I wore gloves during the entire process. For the reminder of the trip, I just thought about how she deserved to die. She was making nothing out of her life. Her parents had given her a chance but she had made no attempt to make herself a better person."

It amazed me that old Blueberry Hill whose life would soon be gone, could sit there and calmly "confess" to such a crime. The "good" thing BH remembered about that trip was that his uncle gave him a thousand dollars for his work. His uncle also told him that the man who owned the dealership in New York had called and wanted BH to call him at the dealership.

"Did this make you nervous?" I asked.

"It really did," he said. "Everything went through my mind about why he had called. I wondered if I might have dropped something belonging to the girl. I knew if I didn't call him back I would never know for sure.

"I made the call and was relieved that he only wanted to know if I would be interested in going to work for a friend of his on Long Island. His friend ran a car restoration shop and needed someone who knew how to work with lead. Lead was used before body filler became popular with all the shops. The pay would be good and I could stay rent-free in a room above the shop.

"When I was in New York getting the cars, I had talked to that guy about my restoration work and how much I loved it. I figured that was why he had called. I thought about the offer for a few days and decided to take it when my uncle was okay with it.

"I still hadn't heard anything about anybody looking for a missing woman from New Orleans, and the gulley was almost full of dirt. I spent a few days fixing up the old van I had used to pick up the body of the first victim and then headed back to New York in the van."

BH slowly mashed his cigar out in the ashtray and reached for another one. These cigars are large and it takes about forty-five minutes to smoke one. He was showing some emotion now and I noticed he was beginning to move one of his feet up and down. I felt that he was getting startled with all the things he had on his mind.

Chapter Three

Duo Teams Up to Rob Johns

As BH talked, I could see the relief in his eyes. He had been carrying all of this on his mind for a long time. Sharing his exploits seemed to be a bit of therapy for the old man. As I suspected, things were about to get a lot worse.

BH resumed his story.

"I moved in above the auto body shop, which gave me a clear view of the harbor across the street. Fishing boats lined the dock and on the other side, were large abandoned warehouses. The apartment was small with one bed and a small bath off to one side. It was all I needed.

"The work was good and I quickly made contacts with other body repairmen in the area. Insurance claims from wrecks were the main supplier of business, but I had projects which allowed me to work on antique cars. I had to split the profits with the owner of the shop, but my clients were mostly old retired guys who wanted to relive their childhood and had plenty of money. It took longer to .fix the old cars but the money was all in cash.

"While looking for some old parts at a nearby junkyard, I met Ralph. He worked in the yard as a mechanic removing parts. We started going out at night and having a few drinks.

"Ralph lived in a small shop in the yard. The rent was free. He also worked as a security guard. Within a few months, Ralph and I became very close."

Ralph interrupted BH to tell us he was fixing some gumbo for supper and that he had brought wine up from the cellar. As soon as Ralph left, BH resumed his story.

"One night coming back from a few hours of drinking and shooting pool, Ralph asked me if I would be interested in making some extra cash.

"He told me that he had been robbing johns (customers of prostitutes). He would wait across the street and watch as johns would drive by and eventually pick up a girl or girls and drive away. He would follow them and usually they would pull into an alley or a vacant parking lot. He would give them a few minutes and walk up to the car, pull a pistol on them, and demand their cash.

"He always kept their driver's license or some type of identification. He would tell the John if they went to the police he would expose them to their wife or employer. It wasn't unusual for him to take in a thousand dollars over the weekend.

"I joined Ralph and we worked as a team robbing the johns.

"This plan worked for me as it had for Ralph. It wasn't long before we were taking in five thousand a month. We decided to split up. Then we could rob twice as many johns as before. It soon reached a point where we really didn't need to work at the body shop and junkyard.

"However, room and board was free so we decided to stay with our employers. This also provided a good cover for what we were really up to.

"Things went really well for about eight months until one of our robberies went wrong. Ralph and I were working the same corner when a big black SUV pulled up. There were two men in the front. They waved their arms out the window and signaled for two girls to come to the vehicle. Two walked over and started talking to them. One of the girls got in but the other one, for some reason, shook her head as if to say no and left.

"We never had robbed a vehicle with two Johns inside. Ralph pulled up beside of me and motioned me to follow him. I never felt good about it from the start and reached down under my seat and pulled out my snub nose .357 Magnum and stuck it in my belt.

"The SUV pulled into a driveway which ran alongside one of the warehouses on the river. Ralph and I drove on by and met at a nearby gas station. Ralph got in the van and we went back to the warehouse.

"We cut the lights and drove by the pole lights near the docks. When we turned the corner, we could see the interior light burning inside of the vehicle. We also could see a woman was in the backseat with one of the men.

"The other man got out of the vehicle and walked down toward the dock. Ralph and I sat there and watched the man and woman who appeared to be making out. Then they disappeared down in the seat.

"After about fifteen minutes, the man at the dock threw his cigarette into the river and made his way back to the car. When he reached the SUV, he tapped on the side glass. A man got out of the left side of the car and the man on the right got in.

"Ralph and I approached with our guns drawn. Ralph yelled out, 'hands up!' The man on the left opened the front door and came out with a gun. I didn't hesitate and fired first and hit him in the chest. The man on the right took off running toward Ralph. Ralph shot him in the face and he quickly fell to the ground.

"The woman in the back seat screamed and tried to get her clothes on. Ralph came back to me and said, 'Get the girl out!' I reached in and grabbed her by the arm and she started begging for me to let her get her clothes on. She looked to be in her early twenties and I knew she didn't need to get her clothes on.

"She offered me sex and said she would do whatever I wanted if I would let her go. As soon as the words came out of her mouth,

I pulled the trigger. The bullet struck her on the left cheek and tore off the whole side of her face. Her hair and brains were hanging on the headliner and the steam from her body heat slowly rose and disappeared out the side window which was down about two inches. I stood and watched as the blood ran down on her bare breast. I liked it.

"Just as I stood up, another round went off and I looked down toward the dock and saw Ralph standing over the other John. He had shot him in the back of the head. We took his body up to the SUV and placed it in the back.

"Then we stuck the first body in the front seat behind the steering wheel. Ralph put the seat belts on the girl and the guy behind the wheel and pulled the car down to the dock close to the water. He said he had worked on the dock years ago and knew the water was very deep along there. He rolled down all of the windows.

"We took fifteen hundred dollars off one guy and over three thousand off the other one. I cranked their car. I raised the hood and used my pocketknife to turn the idle screw a few turns. I closed the hood, put the car in gear, and watched as it drove off the dock about twenty yards away.

"I looked over at Ralph and asked him if we should go down and make sure the vehicle had sunk. He laughed and said, 'What are you going to do? Dive in and sink it?' We left and went back to a bar and had a few drinks."

Listening to BH was like watching the *Goodfellas* movie. What a life this guy had lived. He was without a doubt, the calmest I had ever met. I began wondering how smart I was to be down in the Bayou out in the middle of nowhere with two sick disgusting perverts. The only thing I had for protection was an Army Ka-bar knife strapped to my left leg. I had worm it in Vietnam and on more than one occasion, it had come in handy.

I had a plan for the gumbo. If they tried to serve it to me in a single bowl, I would decline. If we all were served out of the same larger bowl or pot, I would accept it. I wasn't surprised to find out that Ralph was just as crazy as BH, but I was surprised that BH was implicating Ralph in his story.

BH slid his chair back and said, "Sheriff, I notice you aren't writing anything down." I told him I was not there to write a novel. I was there to hear a dying man's last confession. I was no longer a sheriff and I felt that listening to a dying man's last words was something like a lawyer-client privilege or a priest in a confessional. I was fulfilling a promise I had made to his daughter and that was all.

BH nodded as I made my explanation.

The sun was dropping behind the giant magnolias as I looked across the lake and noticed the Irish setter was chasing several wild geese near the dam. It was a peaceful scene, and yet I was sitting here with a diabolical madman who could pass for a loving grandfather. What a life he had lived!

BH stood and told me we would be eating in the grand dining hall. I offered to help him but he wouldn't allow such a thing. Ralph was standing at the two oversized doors, and he pulled them open as we got closer. The opening of the door created a swish of mildewed air.

Inside was a large cherry dining table at least twenty feet long. Again the ceiling was decorated with carvings of magnolia trees and horses. There were mammoth chandeliers at each end of the table. Sixteen chairs, also made of cherry, were neatly placed around the table. The chairs were covered in more of the red velvet I had seen earlier. Encircled with a brass ring near the headrest was the family crest I had first seen at the gate. I really don't know much about decorating but this was impressive to an old country boy from Pilgrim, North Carolina.

I pulled up a chair as Ralph placed a large silver-serving bowl and a tray of yeast bread rolls on the table in front of me. Then he handed me a white china bowl which had a green stripe around the top. On the bottom, was what I guessed to be the family crest. Ralph presented three wine glasses and filled each one. Now I had never had wine with gumbo but wasn't above drinking it.

The gumbo was hot and spicy and once the wine and food were gone, we moved our way into the smoking room. A large and beautiful humidor was visible. It was built into the wall and contained at least fifty boxes of expensive cigars. There were more cherry wood chairs but the seats were covered in black leather that was cracked from years of aging. This room was for men only even though large ferns were in each corner of the room and a single rose in a green vase adorned the center of the large cherry coffee table. I was impressed.

Ralph came over to my chair with a small wooden tray and a selection of three styles of cigars. One was long, one short, and another was long and fat. Beside each cigar were a brass cigar cutter and a silver Zippo cigar lighter, circa 1950. I picked up the long fat one and before I could reach for the cutter, Ralph did the honors. I could tell by the way he handled the lighter he had been around them for a long time.

After I took the first draw, I asked Ralph, "Did you ever work in a restaurant, Ralph?" He turned around with a bottle of French brandy in his hand and said, "No, but I did work as a butler for some time." He said he had also worked in the kitchen while in prison and became so good at it that he was asked to prepare special meals for the prison warden. When it was time for him to be released from prison, the warden got him a job with a rich recluse in Red Bank, NJ. He became his butler, chauffer, and bodyguard for a little over four years. The old man died and Ralph had to go back to the streets.

We sat around and smoked cigars and drank some great brandy while Ralph and BH shared several stories of the early years. Then it was time for BH to resume his death bed story:

"Two week after we shot the people down at the docks, an article came out in the newspaper about a SUV being found in the river. In those days, it was a common thing for cops to find bodies in the river. Other than that small article, we never heard anything about it. It turned out the two guys were known drug dealers and the girl was a local prostitute known to police.

"People who live in small town America don't have a clue about the life of a big city resident. Certain people are considered disposable. Prostitutes, drug dealers, thugs and killers are considered by most of society as being no different than a dead dog in the middle of the road. They all ride by it and tell themselves someone should remove it. They keep driving by it every day. Hundreds, if not thousands, drive by it. Each day the carcass gets worse but they do not stop. Finally, someone calls city officials and demands someone remove it. As long as it disappears, they are happy disgusting little taxpayers.

"Once we robbed a John and a week later I saw his picture on the front page of the newspaper. Come to find out he was a member of the State House of Representatives. It's funny what kind of people you find picking up hookers on the street corners. Police and civic leaders really don't care if the scum of the city is removed as long as they don't have to play a part in it.

BH's energy seemed exceptional as he continued to talk. He was suffering from cancer but wasn't about to slow down until his confession was completed:

"I stayed in New York for about two years and built a small nest egg and then after reading an article in a hunting magazine, I decided I would move down to Texas. I packed up the old van and drove down to El Paso. As usual, I made contacts with local auto repair shops and rented a bay in one of them. The guy I rented from told me about a small ranch outside of town. It had a large barn and the house had just been refurbished

"The owner of the farm and I reached an agreement. In lieu of paying rent, I would maintain the equipment and feed about ten head of cattle. The owner of the farm was retired and he and his wife were going to travel around the world for about a year.

"Within three months, I had several customers at the shop and even brought one of the cars out to the farm. I cleaned out the shop

27

and turned it into a working body shop. By summer, I gave up the bay and was doing everything out at the farm.

"I pretty much kept to myself and never gave anyone my real name. I used different first names.

"There was a row of nightclubs and bars along the highway just outside of El Paso. I went down on weekends and shot pool. One Saturday night in a bar called the Blue Duck, I met some Mexicans while shooting pool. They were driving a low rider truck with a very nice paint job. One thing led to another and before I knew it, we were smoking pot and talking car stuff. After a couple times hanging out, they asked if I would be interested in making hidden compartments in their cars and trucks. They wanted to use the compartments to hide drugs and guns.

"We cut a deal and agreed on a thousand bucks. I did the work and before I knew it, I had Mexicans coming out of the woodwork. I had picked up the Spanish language by dealing with them at the shops where I had worked. I could make out about ninety percent of what they said.

"After I had done about twenty-five of the cars and vans, I told the Mexicans I wasn't interested in doing any more work for them. They were not happy and indicated they no longer trusted me; they were afraid I might go to the police. I thought to myself, if they only *knew*. As they were leaving I overheard one of them say, in Spanish, 'We will come back tonight and make sure he does not talk'.

"I took a shotgun the owner of the ranch had in his home, and I went out to the barn. The terrain around the barn was flat and from the barn I could see for a mile.

"Around midnight I saw one of the vans I had worked on coming down the road. Lights were out on the van. They parked behind the barn and emerged with two long guns and headed toward the house. I watched as they kicked the door in. As soon as they went into the house, I came down from the barn loft. I could hear them cursing in the house. I waited behind a small tool shed near the van.

"Between the cracks of the boarded barn wall, I could see them inside searching for me. In a few minutes they came back to the van. They stood there side by side yelling at each other. I stepped from behind the shed and shot both of them with one round. The blast knocked one to the ground and the other man ran a few feet and fell. I walked up and put another round in each one.

"I looked through the van and found several pistols and an AR-15 rifle. I put all the weapons into my van. The bodies were loaded into their van. I drove them about five miles down the road and left the van at a small shopping mall. Beside the mall was a car repair shop. I figured the van would sit there for a while until someone realized it wasn't there to be worked on. Fortunately, in those days you didn't have cameras on every building.

"I walked back to the ranch and cleaned up the mess behind the barn. I stayed on the ranch for about three months before contacting the owner and advising him I was moving on. He never asked for my ID and never knew my real name."

At that point BH stopped to take a drink, and said, "Sheriff, we have made arrangements for you to spend the night here. You can sleep upstairs or there is small guesthouse on the other side of the lake. I think you would like it out there."

He was right; I don't think I wanted to stay under the same roof with these two killers. I felt no fear but with the stuff I had listened to for the last few hours, I was ready to get a little space between us.

I walked over the small bridge, which led to the guesthouse. Then I walked across the dam and over another small bridge right onto the front porch. Two old milk cans were placed on each side of the nine-pane wooden door. It was an old log house, which had been updated in recent years. I could see a new breaker box on the sidewall, an indication it had been rewired. When I opened the door, the first thing I noticed was a very large grandfather clock next to the stone fireplace. My uncle who worked at the furniture factory for nearly forty years used to make them.

By the obvious movement of the pendulum which also had the family crest on the bottom, the clock was operating well. The hardwood floor was made out of twelve-inch wide forest pine. The pine had turned black over the years which gave it an aged rustic look. The kitchen-living room combination area was accented by a white marble sink and backsplash.

To the left was a bathroom that had an old lion foot tub with brass fittings. There also was a showerhead with a lion's head. The bedroom had a single bed and a cherry four-poster bed. The place was nice and had a large bay window providing a beautiful view of the lake.

The most unique feature of the house was the wagon wheel light fixture which hung from the bead board ceiling. What made the wheel unique was that it had candles instead of bulbs. A rope that ran over to the side of the fireplace could be used to lower and raise the light fixture.

After taking a hot shower, I lowered the light and lit all of the candles. I just had to do it! In the refrigerator, I found a pitcher of ice tea and, of all things, a package of liver pudding. Somehow, BH or his daughter must have done some research and discovered I loved the stuff. This was homemade from a local grocer. It had onions and hot pepper. Man, I was in heaven! There also was a tray of hoop cheese, the kind I'd had when I was a small boy. On the counter was a sleeve of fresh crackers. This old man was riding high.

I built a small fire and sat back in the large black leather recliner. With a small glass of brandy and a fine cigar, I laid back and let all the stories I had heard today just soak in.

Now I was dealing with two sick but intelligent people. I knew nothing of Ralph and wondered. Looking out the window, I could see the Irish setter making one last run at the mallard ducks across the dam. His beautiful red coat was highlighted by the reflection of the moon resting high above the magnolias.

This was such a peaceful place, and it was a sharp contrast to the two sick men who were occupying the place. With all the killings I had been told about today, I knew for everyone they told me about there probably were ten more he didn't tell about. On the other hand, I felt deep inside he was about to divulge them to me.

BH was getting a lot of things off his mind. He was dying and knew even if I would turn him in, he would be dead before anything could develop. On the other hand, Ralph would still be around and possibly would face investigation. I guess both of them are banking on me giving my word to keep it all to myself. And that's what I had done.

Before I went to bed, I took old newspapers used to start the fires and wrinkled them up and placed them on the floor from the door back to the bedroom door. If I had any visitors, the paper just might wake me when they walked on them. I took to the bed and was out in no time.

Around 2 a.m. I was awakened by the sound of the clock chiming with two strikes of the bell. It took me a few seconds to get my breath back. I went into the room and stopped the pendulum.

I slipped back in bed and soon was sleeping comfortably. Sometime later, I was awakened by the movement on the newspapers I had placed on the floor. The house was completely dark. I took a deep breath and listened for the movement. I had used this procedure a thousand times in the war. I slowly reached over and grabbed my K- Bar war knife. Very quietly, I slid off the bed and moved into the corner nearest the door.

If someone entered I was going to attack him or her from behind and cut their throat, pull them down, and stab their lower back. As I waited, the sweat started to run down my back. The movement stopped but I could now hear breathing. It sounded as if someone was just standing there taking a breath as if they were waiting to calm down. I waited about a minute before easing back toward the nightstand where I picked up a small light. I carry a mini-light with me when I travel just in case I have a flat tire or something. After taking my position back behind the door, I made a decision to wait a few seconds and then take the offensive.

Just as I was about to charge out in the large room, I heard the breathing resume at a much faster pace. I knew they were close, maybe in the doorway. I tightened my grip on the knife and prepared for the confrontation about to begin. I switched on the light and made my turn around the door. There right in front of me with his auburn eyes reflecting all the light back to me, calm and breathing very hard, was the Irish setter, tongue hanging out and looking at me as if to say, "What's wrong?" On my knees, knife in hand, I just looked at him and said, "You know you just about gave me a heart attack."

We both went back to the recliner and spent the rest of the night by the warm fire. My life has been filled with some very bad times and some wonderful times, and I started to reflect on my past mistakes while trying to embrace my last years with the hopes of a healthy future. There's nothing likes the comfort of an old dog to make one appreciate the wonderment of life.

As I prepared to go back to the big house, I noticed a trap door near the fireplace. It was used to hand wood inside to the fireplace. I looked at the setter and said, "This is how you got in here last night you, smart dog you." He followed me outside and then made a dash toward the ducks.

When I reached the big house, Ralph had prepared breakfast and had it waiting in what they used to call the labor room. Back in those days, the field hands weren't allowed to eat in the main house. This room was a dining and kitchen combination.

On the old black cast iron wood stove was a pan of eggs being fried sunny-side up. Another pan had large pieces of country ham floating in about an inch of good old fat grease. A bowl of red eye gravy was sitting on the table beside of a big blue bowl of grits. Inside the white ceramic oven door were a dozen homemade biscuits. Mercy, regardless of how I felt about Ralph, the man could cook.

After breakfast, I joined BH out on the back porch. He was still in the same bathrobe and was eating a piece of fruit. "Sheriff, I hope you know how much I appreciate you spending time with me and listening to all of these bad things," BH said as he took a sip from a large cup of coffee.

Ralph placed a large cup of orange juice on the table beside me. BH didn't wait for me to eat before resuming his story:

"I stayed in New York for another year until some of the guys in the shop started talking about a friend who was a detective on the police force. The detective told them that he was investigating a case involving some people being found dead in a car in the river. Police didn't have much to go on, he said. I decided I would hang around about a month longer before moving on.

"I had an old prison buddy who was living near Tampa, Florida. I contacted him and he told me to come on down. He was working at a boat marina and had a small house on the inland waterway that I could use. This sounded perfect for me and in a few days, I was pulling up to the marina.

"Willie and I had pulled two years federal time together in Atlanta for making, selling, and transporting moonshine whiskey. It was easy time and we made a lot of contacts. Pulling time in a federal prison is like going to Harvard Law School. You meet a lot of white-collar criminals. Bankers, lawyers, businessmen, you name it. Even though they are well educated and speak better than we do, they're just like us. They're trying to beat the system."

Chapter Four

Crimes Grow More Bizarre

"Willie took me out to a small fishing cabin on the river. It was small but it had a pier and small motorboat. Willie had plenty of work around the marina -- small engine repair and fiberglass work on the larger boats. As always, introduction to all the bars was first thing on the agenda.

"I was there for about six months until I started to fall back into my bad ways. I was coming out of one of the bars and noticed two women across the street trying to change a flat tire. One was in her fifties and the other one was her daughter who looked to be in her mid-twenties. They told me they were from New Hampshire and were down here for a week of mother and daughter time.

"They thanked me as I finished changing the tire. As I was walking off, they asked if I knew of anyone who could take them out on a snorkeling trip. I told them that I knew someone and gave them a number to call at 9 a.m. the next day. I told them they must call at 9 o'clock sharp if they wanted to get booked. I told them they would be picked up and taken down to the dock around 10:30 a.m. They thanked me and I left.

"The thought of taking these two women to my cabin really turned me on and I prayed they would actually call the number. The number belonged to a pay phone near the dock.

"The next morning the call came in at exactly nine. I answered by saying, 'Tampa Boat and Diving. Bob speaking.' It was the older lady. She fell for it and booked a half-day trip, and I advised her I would pick her and her daughter up at the motel where she was staying.

"Willie had a real nice van he used to take people to the airport on the weekends. It had nice lettering on the side which read 'Bay Shuttle.' I would use it during the week to pick up parts.

"I told him I needed the van and he had no problem with it. I proceeded to pick up the women and placed their small bags in the rear of the van. I had a roll of duct tape and my pistol in a black bag under the seat. After the pickup, I drove to my cabin and told the women I had to go by there and pick up some tools for the boat.

"With no houses nearby, the cabin was rather isolated at the end of a dirt road. I pulled around to the back of the cabin and told them I would be right back.

"I grabbed the bag and headed to the side door of the van. When I opened the door, the older women asked me what was going on. I pulled the pistol and told both of them to shut up, turn around, and put their hands behind their backs. The older woman said, 'Please don't hurt us. Take whatever you want.' I said, 'Don't worry lady. I will.'

"I bound their hands behind them with the duct tape. The young girl was crying and talking to God. I put tape over their mouths and told them to walk around to a shed near the river.

"The shed had originally been used to raise minnows for the fishermen. It had two septic tanks, and each was about eight feet in length. Both had air supplies and hinged wooden tops. I made them get in one and lie down. I locked both of the tanks with padlocks. I cut the small compressor on and left for the dock. I had to get Willie's van back in order not to make him suspicious. Willie was trying to go straight and I knew I could not trust him."

I held my hand up and signaled for BH to stop and then asked him, "When you decide to do these things, do you just do them off the cuff or do you have a plan beforehand?"

"No, I plan things as they happen." He said, "That's what makes it all the more exciting. There are no disappointments. It's like rape without the body."

I looked at BH and told him to continue.

"I cleaned out the van and returned to the dock to work for the rest of the day. My heart was running wild and I couldn't wait to get back to the girls and spend a night fulfilling all my fantasies

I took a swallow of iced tea and thought about how this man was so deranged. Dying a slow death was appropriate for him.

When we resumed the conversation, I asked BH if he had any concern about how the women back at his house were suffering while he was working. The fact that they were bound with duct tape and in a dark concrete pit seemed pretty awful, I said.

He looked at me with those cold blue eyes and said, "Nope, not one time. They were just objects to me. It's like tying your old dog to a fence post. You hate to do it, but if you don't, he will run away."

BH continued with his "confession:"

"After work I went by the bar and stayed until dark. I went back to the house and then out to the shed. I opened the door to the mother's side first. She was lying on her back and looking straight up at me. I could see the fear in her eyes. I pulled her out and carried her inside the house to the bathroom. I could see she had soiled herself during the day. I cut on the shower and removed the tape. I put my pistol to her head and told her to take her clothes off and take a shower.

"I sat on the toilet and watched her bathe. She was crying and mumbling some words. I told her to speak up and she then told me she was just asking God to help her through this. I told her God wasn't going to help her or anyone else. I asked her why she thought God was going to help her. She kept crying. I reached in the shower and grabbed her around the neck and asked if she thought God was going to break down the door and come in here and take my gun.

"Did she think any of her friends were going to save her? I slapped her in the face and she slid down in the shower and started throwing up. I kicked her in the chest and told her to get out and dry off. She got out and started to put a towel around her and I jerked it away. I then told her to dry off and put the towel back on the rack.

"When she finished, I took her back to the kitchen and put her in a chair with a high back. Then I bound her with tape. She asked if she could have something to drink. I walked over to the cabinet and got a bottle of bourbon and put it in front of her. She told me she did not drink and I told her, 'You do now!'

"I stuck the bottle to her lips and made her take several swallows. I could tell she was not a drinker and probably was a Bible thumper.

"I went back out to the shed and brought the girl in the house. I took her to the shower and told her to clean up and then she could join the party. She had a nice young body and long hair. I watched her and even washed her back.

"After she finished I took her into the kitchen with her mother. I made them drink for about an hour. The girl was much more tolerant to the whiskey. She may have been a Bible thumper, but I could tell it wasn't her first drink of whiskey.

"I walked around the table and started kissing their necks and stroking their hair. The mother started begging me to take her and not hurt her daughter. I laughed and told her I was going to take both of them at the same time.'

I pushed my chair back and asked BH, "What was the point of all the verbal bashing? You knew you were going to kill both of them."

BH picked up his lighter and tapped the table top. "You see, Sheriff. People like me are never known for anything. We are put here on earth so people like you have a job. Have you ever thought how many people would be out of work if it weren't for people like me? All those prison guards, cops, judges, lawyers and preachers wouldn't be needed.

"What if one day we all just woke up and everyone was walking around with a lollipop and soda. All the houses were white. Hell, we wouldn't need traffic lights because everyone would be so nice. They would let their fellow men go first. People like me generate millions of jobs for the whole judicial society.

"I decided long ago I was going to be one of those people who provided jobs for all of those high and mighty people who look down their noses at the rest of the world. They don't care about how bad things are as long as something doesn't happen to them.

"Sheriff, remember when you had your problems and had to resign? Do you remember all those people you helped and all those days you went without sleep to help people? How about the chases, the shootouts, and putting your life on the line every single day? I know you haven't forgotten.

"Well, let me ask you this, Sheriff, How many of those good people came down your driveway and offered you help? Let me guess. No more than five. Just like these five fingers right here on my hand -- the very hand that has reached around the throats of all those good folks and squeezed the life out of them.

"Those people gave me the same amount of help as they did you. That is why I wanted you to come down here and listen to a dying, low-life killer. Because we have a lot more in common than you might think."

I could tell he wanted me to respond but I knew it would just take up more time. I had dealt with people like this before. They want someone to prove them wrong. They want an argument or at least some sort of verbal combat. In my day, I was known as one of the best at that art form. That's behind me. I wanted to hear more BH.

Ralph came out and brought us a mimosa drink. A little too

feminine for me but I took it anyway. Ralph took a seat to my left and for the first time, he lit up a cigar and said, "Sheriff, BH has a hell of a memory doesn't he?"

I took a sip of the girly drink and said, "Yes, he sure does." These guys talked about killing and torture as though they had been to a family reunion and were discussing all the people they had not seen for years.

BH put down his glass and resumed:

"I took my clothes off and pulled up another chair and just sat there and watched the mother and daughter crying. I placed drinking glasses on the table and poured each of them a drink. I made them drink for about thirty minutes. I could tell they were getting drunk because the crying stopped. The longer I looked at them, the more I wanted to kill them. They were pathetic; they had lived a sheltered life and knew nothing of the real world.

"I walked over to the drawer beside the sink and pulled out a sixteen-ounce claw hammer; and walked over to the mom and bashed in her skull. Blood splattered all over her daughter's face and she fell backwards to the floor. The mother fell face down on the table. When I went to the other side of the table, the girl got up and tried to hop with the chair to the door. I returned to the cabinet and found a large carving knife. I started cutting the girl's long hair. To stop her screaming, I stuck the knife in her mouth and pulled her into the bathroom. There I put her in the bathtub and stabbed her about twenty five times. She passed out and I cut the shower on and let it run while I went back to the mom.

"A large piece of mom's skull was on the table. I picked it up and put it in the sink. I grabbed the bottle of whiskey and went into the living room and watched a movie. I smoked a cigarette and listened to the water running in the shower. After the movie, I started cleaning up the mess I had created. I took both bodies out to the tanks and closed the lids.

"The next day during my lunch break, I took the van down an old logging road to an old mill. I filled the back of the van with sawdust. I went by the house and covered the bodies with sawdust, and returned to my job. That evening I went back for more sawdust and filled the tanks within two feet from the top. I bought a few bags of planting soil at Walmart. Two days later while I was at the tanks spreading more dirt, Willie pulled up. He walked down to the shed and asked, 'What you doing? Getting ready to raise night crawlers?' Without missing a beat, I replied, 'That is exactly what I am doing.'

"The next day I bought 200 night crawlers.

"For the next year, I sold night crawlers down at the dock. One day I saw a story on TV about two missing women. Since it had been over a year, I figured it was doubtful they had any suspects. Anything about suspects probably would have been part of the story. The fact that no one had been around the dock asking questions told me I should be safe. I worked with Willy another six months before telling him it was time for me to move on. In our circles, no one ever asks why."

Chapter Five

Truck Stop Adventure

That was about all I wanted to hear for now. It was time for a break. I motioned to BH that I needed to step outside. He nodded okay. I stood, stretched, and looked for the dog. He was at the lake, so I walked over to the bridge and yelled for him to come. He came and sat beside me. While I rubbed his head, I said, "Boy, I hope you know you are living with two crazy SOBs. I feel for you and wish I could take you with me." He put his paw on my knee and waited for another pat on the head.

When I returned to the table, Ralph had placed a large coffee table album at my seat. Opening it, I immediately recognized it was a Sheriff Crawford scrapbook. When I looked up at Ralph, he said, "See, Sheriff. We have been keeping up with you for a long time. We even have several VHS tapes of your show." Page after page of articles and photos had been collected. Most of the stories were about the 25 murder cases I had worked and solved.

Ralph sat down beside me and said that after BH left my jail, he would call and tell him to collect articles and anything else he could find about me. They both loved the TV show and watched reruns of the shows I did on "Cops."

I looked over at BH and asked, "So where did you go after you left Tampa?"

41

He called for the dog, and began:

"I left Tampa with plenty of cash and decided to head out west. I had never been to Vegas and knew with all the car repair people out there I wouldn't have any problem finding a little work. I also knew there would be plenty of women and johns.

I could start robbing the johns like as I had done in New York.

"Another thing I liked about Nevada was that prostitution was legal, and the guys who take the junkets out there are looking for pleasure. Men don't go to Vegas without their wives just to gamble.

"I stopped at a truck stop on I-40 a few miles east of Albuquerque, New Mexico. At least a hundred trucks were parked around the very large lot. It was one of those travel centers where they have the family atmosphere on one side and the truckers on the other. I had been driving for about fifteen hours and decided to go inside and take a shower.

"After the shower, I went to the counter and paid for a fill-up for the van. While at the counter, I noticed a woman in her forties buying cigarettes. She was a short lady with a nice build. She also had red hair. That is what got me excited; I wanted to have a red headed woman. I watched as she went outside and headed for a motor home parked at the far end of the lot. Several of the night-lights were burned out in that area and she disappeared to the back of the coach.

"I pulled my van down closer to her coach and cut off the lights. As she came around the corner of the coach she was lighting a cigarette. When the lighter lit, it created a glow on her face. I could see her high cheekbones and her long hair hanging down on her shoulders. It turned me on and I knew I wanted her.

"It looked like she was going to open the door but then she went back to a storage compartment on the side of the coach. She opened the door and pulled out a long bar. She also had a flash light in her other hand. She started checking all the tires on the camper by hitting them to see if they were low. I knew the procedure very well. I also knew she could use the bar as a weapon.

"I got back into my van and rode around the parking lot looking for security cameras. Cameras were only on the pumps, and I knew then that I would be okay. When I got back to the motor home, the woman was putting the bar back into the side compartment. I got out of the van and raised the hood. I would use this for a way to start a conversation.

"I walked over to her and asked if I could borrow her flashlight to check my battery cables. She walked over to me and said, "Well sure. I have some wrenches if you need some." At this moment I knew she wasn't scared. She returned to her camper and went inside, cranked it up and turned on the lights. It was a Pusher type motor home with the motor in the rear. They are expensive, and this meant she might have some traveling money on board.

"I'm always amazed how stupid people are. You would think people would know better than to talk to a stranger in a big dark parking lot. What is the first thing every parent tells his or her kids? 'Don't talk to strangers.' It was the human side of people which enabled me to get the upper hand.

"I messed around my van to make her think I really had a problem. I opened the door and got my pistol and duct tape and headed back to the coach.

"I knocked at the door of the bus, and she opened the door. "'Returning your tools,' I said. I went inside and she asked me about the problem and I told her it was the battery. She was sitting in the driver's seat checking the gauges on the dash. I thanked her and turned as if I were leaving. She said, 'You're welcome' and I turned around and pointed the pistol at her.

"Unlike most of my victims, she didn't show any emotion. She looked me right in the eye. 'What do you want? I have no money,' she said.

"Cut the engine and lights off, and get up," I said. She got up and looked at me. I told her to go to the back of the bus into the bedroom. I followed her back and looked at the little floor lights which ran along the bottom of the cabinets. It gave off just enough light to show off her feet and legs. She had nice legs. Her jeans were tight fitting, the way I like them. She was large boned but not too heavy.

"When we reached the bedroom, I noticed a little night light, the kind you plug into a wall socket. It gave off enough light to see her face and I could see her long eyelashes moving up and down. She was beautiful. The sound of the generator was driving me crazy but I knew I better leave it on. I didn't want to take the chance of walking to the front of the bus.

"I never had seen anyone this calm before. She hadn't spoken a word since we reached the bedroom. She looked right at me; and didn't show any fear. I moved over and placed the barrel of the gun on her lips and moved it down her cheek.

"While I moved to a corner of the bedroom, I told her to undress. A large mirror on the wall made the procedure even better. I could see her shadow on the wall created by the night-light. She took off her top and started to remove her jeans.

"I started to remove my belt when there was a knock on the side of the camper. 'Honey, open the door, what are you doing?' came a man's voice. I grabbed her by the red hair and asked her 'Who the hell is that?' She looked up and said, 'It's my boyfriend. The shower in the camper isn't working and he went inside to take a bath.' I told her to tell him to wait a minute.

"As soon as she said, 'be there in a minute,' I put tape over her mouth and bound her legs. I had noticed when I came inside the camper she had already pulled the night curtains shut. There also was a curtain on the door. Lucky for me, her boyfriend had walked toward the back for some reason. I hit the door button and went back to the small bath in the hallway.

"I shut the bedroom door and stepped back into the small bath. In less than a minute, I could hear footsteps coming down the hall. He said, 'What are you doing? Let's go get something to eat.'

"I could feel him getting closer. When he passed the door, I jumped out and hit him in the back of the head. He went down and before he could get up, I hit him several more times. He was a small man and was wearing a white dress shirt. I could see the blood running down his neck. The blood was bleeding through the shirt.

"He tried his best to get up but I kept beating him in the head. Finally, he passed out with his head lying at the woman's feet. For the first time, I could see fear in her eyes. I knew it would be too risky to shoot them. Although there was a lot of noise coming from the several big diesel engines idling nearby, I figured someone pumping gas might hear a gun shot.

"I pulled my belt off and pulled the woman off the bed. I told her to bend down beside her boyfriend. I could hear her saying 'please' under the duct tape. I used my lighter to take a look at the boyfriend. I could see that his skull was cracked and he was not breathing. The woman started crying. I took the belt and choked her until she passed out and fell on top of the boyfriend.

"She was still breathing, so I went to the kitchen and got a knife and slit her throat. I watched as she bled out. It was exciting to watch.

"I thought about going into the kitchen and putting on a frying pan of grease and heating it until it burst into flames. However, this would have created a lot of attention. I knew it would take a couple days before anyone would check the camper. Hell, it could take a week and I would be long gone.

"The boyfriend had five hundred bucks in his wallet. I took the cash and left the generator running. This would make people think someone was inside resting. I left the camper and went back to the van and headed out for Vegas. All I could think about was how stupid people are."

I knew from being a sheriff of a rural county in North Carolina that this killer had probably preyed upon runaways. He fit the profile because he liked to dominate weaker people. Most people who reported a missing child or young adult always had something in common. The first thing out of their mouths would be, "My child would not run away from home. I know something is wrong." There was something wrong, all right. It was the fact they did not want to admit they, as parents, had failed to see all the signs. Someone living in a good world just doesn't want to leave it.

I don't remember one runaway case where I failed to find and return a minor child. I did have cases where I found the location of legal age young adults who were doing fine and didn't want to go back home.

Here's an example of a common runaway case that may surprise people:

A woman came to me about her runaway daughter. She knew she had run away because she was dating a much older man. Her daughter was sixteen at the time. The man was forty years old. I asked why in the world she allowed her daughter to date a man who was old enough to be her father. Her reason? "Well, he seemed to be a nice guy and had a good job." I asked, "How long had you, the mother, known this nice guy, before you, the mother, let your daughter date him?" She pulled a tissue out of her purse and started crying. "My daughter told me she was dating this nice guy she had met at a friend's house. She had dated him for about a month before he came to the house."

It was moments like these when I had to restrain myself from jumping across the table and spanking people like this mother. I don't have a daughter but I can only imagine my reaction if I opened my door and a 40-year-old man was standing there to pick up my 16-year-old daughter. I would beat him all the way to his car. I would then bend my daughter over my knee and spank her.

Missing person cases were always serious matters to me. Unfortunately, most of these cases are seen as a pain in the ass for law enforcement. The investigations take a lot of time and usually result in finding the child with a friend or relative. Many times I had people come to see me even though they didn't live in my jurisdiction. I looked at every case as though it involved one of my own children. I developed an investigation template to go by in regards to reacting to the initial report.

The media can play an important part in the recovery of missing people, especially in finding children. The quicker law enforcement can get a picture of the missing person circulated, the more likely someone will respond with a tip that may be helpful in locating the missing person. However, soon after a missing person report is circulated, there seems to be little interest by the public to maintain interest in a case. Most people who see missing person stories on TV and pictures of children on milk cartons, take a quick glance and aren't moved. This is sad, but very true.

I had one rule concerning complaints or reported crimes and concerns from the public. I called it my "Mailbox to Murder rule." I took everything seriously as though it were happening to me.

I listened to the mother of the missing girl for about an hour. I located the girl in New Orleans, and she actually was 18 years old. She had left home because her mother had harped on her about being fat. She had a job and was living with a relative. I checked it all out and the case was closed. I never heard from the mother again.

Chapter Six

Disloyal Enforcer Kills Again

Ralph brought us more fruit and BH began another story:

"Once I reached Vegas, I went to an auto parts store and asked if they knew of any local restoration shops that might be hiring. They gave me several tips but the one that caught my eye concerned an old man who lived about ten miles outside of Vegas. He had a small shop but always had work.

"I found that shop and saw that it once had been a Shell gasoline station. It had three bays and the gas pumps had been removed. Several antique cars were scattered around the lot. '35, '40 and '50 Ford coupes were lined around the side of the building. The shop owner emerged from the back of the shop. With his white curly hair and white beard, he looked like he was ninety years old. I could tell, even though I didn't see any bikes, he was an old biker dude. Tattoos and a large scar on his face just screamed, "Bad ass."

"We talked a while and he gave me a job. I went to work on a '40 Ford coupe that very day. The shop owner had an old camper in the back, and I put my stuff in it and spent the evening getting the stove and shower working. The fewer people I had contact with was all by design. I gave the old man a fake name and from his appearance and language, he probably could not have cared less.

"After about three weeks working there, I could tell that the shop owner might be old but he had a bigger business than fixing old cars. A lot of people were coming into the shop that had never walked by a wrench, let alone had actually used one.

"The customers were driving BMWs and Jaguars, and most of them were foreigners. Many were from Japan or China. They always went into the office with the old man and acted as if I wasn't even there. I knew it would be only a matter of time until the old man would bring me in on the action. I had been in the game too long to start asking questions.

"After about two months, the old man finally asked me to ride with him to look at an old car. It was on a weekend night. We took the black '34 Ford coupe and headed toward the strip in Vegas. Two miles outside of town the old man took a sharp left and pulled up to a gated house. He put in the code to open the gate and eased the car up the driveway. When we reached the house, I was surprised to see the size of the place.

"The house was big; I mean BIG! It was done in Spanish villa style. It was, like most of the nice homes around Vegas, pink in color with perfect landscaping and fountains. He raised one of the four garage doors to reveal a nice black Mercedes-Benz S-Class sedan. Those babies run around a hundred thousand dollars or more. I knew right then we would not be drinking Budweiser.

"We went inside and the place was unreal. Big white columns, beige walls and white marble, an indoor pool, and billiard room filled the place. A Mexican guy dressed in a white jacket and black tie was behind a large horseshoe shaped bar.

"The old man motioned me to come over to the bar. 'Well, what do you think?' he said. Hell, I didn't know what to think and for sure wasn't going to ask the old man whose house it was.

"He handed me a glass of Crown Royal. The house was his, he said. We walked down a large hallway and into a big room in the back. A Mexican woman was waiting. The old man told her to show me the bedroom and assist me in getting ready. The woman seemed to be in her fifties and asked me to come in and take a shower. She laid some clothes on the bed and said she would be back in about twenty minutes. When I got out of the shower, the woman was there to tell me to get dressed with the clothes on the bed and meet the old man back at the bar.

"I never had worn clothes like this in my life. The closet was bigger than any place I had ever lived. I didn't know what was going on but I liked it so far.

"The old man was waiting at the bar and told me to follow him. We went out to the garage, and another Mexican man was waiting beside the Mercedes and was dressed in a chauffer's uniform. The old man followed the code; never tell anyone's name unless it's necessary.

"We left the villa and headed for the strip down in Vegas. The old man and I sat in the back seat. From the bar in the back seat, we drank some more Royal. I couldn't believe how the old man had transformed his appearance. He looked like a movie star you may have seen in the movie "Scarface." Even the scar on the left side of his face made him look good, but tough. His speech also had changed. I just couldn't believe I was with the same man who hours earlier had been covered with body filler dust.

"We got down to the strip and the old man had the driver pull into a parking lot, which connected to the strip. We pulled up to the gate, and a man came out and said, 'Hello boss.' The old man said he also owned the parking lot. We parked facing the street and the old man told the driver to get out and find something to do.

"He poured each of us a glass of Royal and asked, 'What do you see out there on the streets?' I could see the usual mass of tourists and gamblers moving like cows down the sidewalk. 'A lot of people, lots of suckers trying to beat the odds,' I said.

"You are right," he said. "Look over at the corner and tell me what you see." I told him I could see a bunch of young girls dressed in miniskirts.

"He rolled down the window. 'What you see are young teenage girls, who have run away from home. They are running away from the law or a sick father or relative who has molested them since they were ten years old. Some are poor and most of them are black. They're a picture of the world we live in,' he said. 'Some even have good parents who love them but are too busy doing their own thing to see the problem. They are missing and no one gives a crap about them, and eventually they don't give a crap about themselves.

'Look at the so-called good people who are walking by them. They take a quick glance and then move on to their nice hotel. It's as though they think something is going to rub off on them.

"Those same good people go back to their fancy rooms, get drunk, get naked and do the same things as they suspect and condemn the girls for what they are forced into doing. The good folks then fly back to good town USA and return to being soccer moms and bankers, preachers and I-love-my-kids mom and dads.

"The girls across the street get into cars with strangers and do things they don't want to do. Just think how bad their lives must have been at home to make them put their miserable lives on the line," he said.

"Man, the old man was getting deep into all the people on the strip. I couldn't tell if he was preaching or just mad. He then went on to tell me his point.

"This is where I come in. I am the one who will take them from making twenty-dollars for a trick to making two hundred dollars to five hundred dollars a trick. I am the one who will take them from sleeping with some lowlife in a cheap hotel to sleeping with a rich Jap or Chinese dude in a five-hundred-dollars-a-night room at the Bellagio."

"The old man was really getting into his rant about the girls but I really didn't give a crap about anyone's feelings. Just tell me what is in it for me. He finally asked if I would work the strip for him and collect the money from the clients. Not to be a pimp but to be a bagman for the pimps. In other words, I would be the enforcer who picked up the money for the old man and if the pimps didn't have it, break an arm or two.

"It took the old man about two weeks to show me all of the

ins and outs of the routine. Of course, I fell right in. The old man would be at the shop every day and back at the villa at night. I met the pimps back at the shop around two in the morning to pick up the money. It was always in a locked brief case. I never had the combination.

"There was an old 55-gallon barrel at the side of the store. It had a fake top which held about five gallons of water. It was my job to put the brief cases in the barrel, replace the top, and refill it with water. Most of the pimps were Chinese except for one very large black woman. She was over six feet tall and at least two hundred pounds. She was one ugly woman, and her arms were bigger than my own. I could tell she didn't like me, and the feeling was mutual.

"The old man paid me two thousand dollars a week to collect the money. With the kind of money I was making, I knew I could move to a better place than the old camper behind the shop. I stayed in the camper because I didn't want the attention. Money meant nothing to me. I knew I would blow it on drugs anyway. I also knew it was only a matter of time until I would steal some of the old man's money and hit the road. He made the mistake of trusting me. Like all the rest, even though he had millions, I knew we were from the same cloth. Eventually, he would have to get rid of me because I knew too much. This wasn't my first rodeo.

"Another three months came and went before I decided to prepare to get out of Vegas. I decided to go down to the strip and check on the pimps and the girls. Several conventions were in town so I knew the girls would be busy. I stopped by the old man's house on the way into town to let him what I was doing. He was by himself. The help had left early and he was out by the pool.

"I took a chair beside him; the only sound was from the large waterfall behind us. He was sitting in his silk robe and slippers, drinking his Royal and smoking a Cuban. We had a few drinks and I told him I was ready to go. About half way to the door he told me to come back.

"He told me he was having problems with the big black lady. She had lied about the action of her ten girls and the number of johns they had seen. She had been stealing from the old man. He said he was afraid she might go to the law if he threatened her. He told me to find someone who could take care of her.

"Of course, I quickly asked him how much it would be worth to him. 'Fifteen-thousand dollars,' he said. I knew I was the man for the job. He gave me half in cash and I left.

"I didn't like the old gal anyway and this could be a lucrative deal for me. I found the big lady in a parking lot sitting in her Cadillac watching her girls. I opened the door and took a seat. She wasn't too happy to see me; I told her the old man wanted us to ride out to the house and meet with him. I could tell by the look on her face she knew what it was about. She told me she would follow me out to his house. I told her the old man wanted me to ride out with her.

"We headed toward the house and she began asking questions about why the old man wanted to see her. Knowing the plans I simply told her I had no idea.

"She said she had some money for the old man out at the shop, and we headed that way. This worked out well for me. Once we arrived I told her I had some good cocaine out in the camper if she wanted to do a line.

"I placed three lines of coke on the table. As she bent over and started to snort a line, I hit her in the head with the pistol. Her head went down and she came right back up and hit me in the face with her elbow. The blow knocked me backwards and she said, 'Why you lowlife son-of-a-bitch, I will rip your eyes out.'

"She went back to the table and reached in her purse and pulled out a can of pepper spray and shot it in my face. I ran toward her and hit her between the eyes with the pistol.

"The spray was burning my eyes but it was not the first time I had been sprayed. In prison, the guards used it on me many times. She went down to her knees but came right back up. She rammed

53

her knee right in my junk and that put me down; and a kick in the face knocked one of my teeth out.

"She was trying to make it to the door when I stuck the pistol in her back and pulled the trigger, and she fell out the door. I turned and went to the sink to wash out my eyes.

"To my surprise when I turned around, she hit me in the head with a car jack that had been sitting near the door. As I going down, I grabbed her around the waist and pushed her back to the door. Both of us fell outside and she landed on top of me, and started punching me in the face. Blood covered her blouse and it seemed like the cocaine was fueling her reaction.

"I was able to roll her over, and I jumped up and went back inside where I had dropped my gun on the floor. I scampered to get the pistol and picked it off the floor. When I looked around, I could see her crawling toward the shop. She stood up once and then fell back to the ground. I ran up behind her and shot her three times in the back.

"I rolled her over again and she spit in my face. 'You piece of shit, you will get yours,' she said. I bent down and put my face about two inches from her face and said, 'No baby, you are getting yours right now.' I put the pistol in her right eye and pulled the trigger.

"I got my stuff, including my tooth, out of the trailer and was ready to hit the road. I looked in her car and found a briefcase in the trunk. I found another briefcase in the barrel.

"I left the big woman on the ground. I knew now I would have to go back to the old man's house and take care of him.

"I rang the doorbell and the old man opened the door. He was still alone and was wearing his smoking jacket. We walked back to the pool and he bent over to get something out of the pool. While he was turning around, he said, 'Was the debt paid in full?'

"I replied, 'Oh Yes!' I shot him in the head and he fell back into the pool. The blood was so heavy it cycled through the skimmer in a matter of seconds.

"To make it look like a robbery, I put my gloves on and went through the house and pulled drawers out and placed them on the floor. I had looked for them before and knew the old man didn't have surveillance cameras. He was too smart for that because he knew the tapes could be used as 'witnesses' against him.

"I didn't look for more money. I knew I had enough. I also knew once the bodies were discovered, nobody would really give a crap. All the cops wanted were both of these people gone. Hell, the cops probably would have a party.

"There was one thing I had to do before I left town. I had been watching one of the girls who worked the corner. Every night around midnight she would leave the corner and walk around to the back of the parking lot and sit in her car for a few minutes. I guess she needed to get away for a few minutes. I parked the van and waited for her to take her break.

"As soon as I saw the car's interior light go on and off, I made my move with a large rag that I had sprayed with starting fluid. I knew she had seen me around enough and probably would roll down her window when she saw me.

"I tapped on her window and she rolled the window down. 'What's up?' she asked.

"The old man is around front and wants to see you," I said. She put her cigarette out and said, 'Holy shit. What in the world for?' She got out of the car and stood up. I grabbed her from behind and put the rag over her face. She was very petite and was no match for me. I pulled the van around and put her in the back. I bound her with the tape and headed out of town. Next stop, Montana."

BH signaled Ralph to come over to the table to assist him in standing up. "Got to take a break, Sheriff. I get a little weak when I talk a long time," he said. This was fine with me.

Chapter Seven

Experiences Made
Him Cold-Hearted

After hearing about all of this carnage, I was ready for a cigar and liver pudding and crackers. I went back to the guesthouse and made the sandwich, grabbed some sweet tea, and headed out to the lake.

As I headed for the dam, I noticed a path leading down into the woods. It came out behind the house where I could see an old lean-to shed. There was a river rock wall underneath under the shed, and it had a large wooden door that had hand-made hinges on it and a twist handle made from solid copper.

I opened the door and could see a long tunnel heading back toward the direction of the house. It reminded me of the old tunnels in an old Boris Karloff movie. The tunnel path split and I took the one to the right. Small forty-watt bulbs located about every twenty feet lit the tunnel. After about fifty feet, it opened up into a large room. It was the wine cellar. Man! It looked to contain somewhere around two to three hundred bottles of wine stored in individual slots. A roll about ladder was hooked to a long rod at the ceiling. A handmade table in the center of the room with four maple chairs provided a place to test the wine.

I sat at the table and enjoyed the sandwich. Looking around

the room, I couldn't help but think about all the victims I had just heard about. How many families are left not knowing the fate of their loved-ones. I also wondered if some of the families even cared. Being in the war and also being a sheriff has made me cold-hearted. I met so many uncaring parents in my life. They spent every moment tending to their own needs and pleasures. That attitude is passed onto the next generation. These selfish traits are handed down from one family to another.

I was out of law enforcement for twenty-years. When I was elected sheriff, I saw people in jail who were members of the same families in which I had made arrests twenty years earlier. Their fathers and grandfathers had been in the same jail. Only a small percentage ever make it out and live stable, normal lives. BH knew this as well and was a prime example of it.

Often I had to reach down deep in my gut and refrain from taking justice into my own hands. I had dreams of living in the Old West and hunting down killers and hanging them from an old scrub oak in the high plains of Kansas. The legal system isn't, nor has it ever been, used as honest people picture it. I'm not talking about the forefathers and the U.S. Constitution. I'm talking about the law of the land.

Those old guys who wrote the Bill of Rights were a group of rich slave owners who made and drank whiskey, raped black female slaves, and fathered children they abandoned or sold off to other rich white farm owners. I'm talking about the men and women who had to fight the battles and shed the blood while those guys lived the good life. Nothing has changed. We just have different old guys drinking whiskey and sending young men and women off to war to die for absolutely nothing.

Police officers are sent out into the streets to be used for target practice while idiots are marching in the same streets calling them killers and racists. I would never survive in the law enforcement business today. These thoughts kind of scare me. I could see where this criminal BH and I had some common thoughts. I figured that

I needed to spend a little time picking his mind in our next session. There were a few things I would like to know for my own peace of mind. Maybe BH was getting into my head.

I had my eyes closed and was in deep thought when I looked up and found Ralph standing in front of me. He scared the crap out of me. He was like a ghost the way he showed up without a sound.

"I see you found the wine cellar, sheriff," he said, as he sat down beside me. I wasn't aware that my cigar had gone out until Ralph reached over and lit it. "Thank you," I said.

"Ralph, you and BH have some bond together. You seem a lot more refined than BH and, like him, you show little or no emotion about anything."

He stood up and said, "Follow me." We went to another room located back toward the entrance door where I had entered. He opened the door and inside was a small auditorium that contained about twenty-five chairs and a small stage. On the stage was a black grand piano. Ralph pointed to a seat in the rear and I sat down. He stepped onto the stage, sat down at the piano, and started playing.

I was blown away. He began playing, "Blueberry Hill." I couldn't believe how great it sounded. I expected Fats himself to walk on stage. This guy was great! When he finished, he began to play "Amazing Grace." These are two of my favorite songs of all time.

He stood and told me the history of the room. The owner of the home had used the room to entertain his guests who would come here and listen to his daughter play music and sing. The owner, though a very wealthy man, was somewhat of a recluse and rarely left the plantation. He had once spent ten years here without once leaving.

Ralph continued his story. "His wife died a mysterious death and people say she haunts the grounds to this day. She was furious at her husband for not allowing her to take part in social functions in the city. The owner built the guesthouse at the lake after she would no longer sleep with him. People who worked here said she was a prisoner of the guesthouse.

"The story was told that she tried to poison him and he became seriously ill. Her plan was to have him taken to the hospital. Then she would be able to leave and go to her sister's house in New York.

"He refused to be taken to the doctor and made sure his butler kept her on the grounds. Knowing he would soon discover her attempt to murder him, she attempted to poison herself but was interrupted by the butler. The butler was persuaded through sex to help her hide her shenanigans."

Ralph asked me to follow him into another room, which was damp and cold. In the center of the room was a circular wall made of rock. Inside and down, was the first original water source for the house. Here was a hand-dug well that reached a depth of forty feet. I could see the foot and hand holds on the walls of the well. When workers dug wells and laid the rock walls, they made slots in the walls in order to be able to climb out. The water was carried over to dumbwaiters and then pulled up to each individual floor where it was dispersed to each room.

Ralph continued. "They found her body in the bottom of the well. On top of her, they found the body of the butler. Both had drowned. The theory at the time was that she was looking over the edge of the wall using a lantern to look at the bottom. She slipped and when the butler, who had become her lover, tried to catch her, he also fell to his death.

"The owner of the plantation, who made large contributions to the local politicians, was never a suspect and the incident was ruled an accident. When we moved into the place, we were told you could hear both of the victims screaming for help. All the help left and the old house sat here for years and years until it finally was sold at auction."

All of this history was fine and dandy but I couldn't find any reason why I had been invited down there. Ralph asked me to follow him outside, and we headed toward the lake. At the dam area, Ralph had already placed a table with a white linen cloth. Two bottles of wine were in the center of the table. At one end of the table sat BH in his wheel chair and waving in my direction.

Several plates on the table were filled with cold cuts and cheese, including liver pudding and crackers. A light breeze was coming from the west which prompted Ralph to place a blue sweater on BH's shoulders.

Although BH was chewing on a grape, he began his story about Montana.

"The reason I went to Montana was to lay low for a few months. An inmate friend of mine had told me about a cabin he had way back in the mountains. It was his father's old place. The inmate was pulling time for shooting at a park ranger who had chased him into the woods for killing elk out of season. We became pretty tight and I knew he hated the government. I also knew it would cost me some hard cash. Prisoners are never good friends. We all have the understanding or the Golden Rule of thugs and thieves, 'What's in it for me?'

"I found a campground right off the interstate and rented a space. I never use one of those chain campgrounds. They ask too many questions. I checked on the girl and she was awake but wasn't trying to break free. I sat her up against the wall of the van and told her if she would be quiet, I would remove the tape from her mouth. She nodded in agreement. After the tape was off she took a deep breath. I knew by her being a hooker that she probably was a tough girl. Hookers' lives aren't like we see in movies. They take a chance at getting hurt every time they take their clothes off.

"She thought the whole deal was some kind of sex deal. She had been involved in a lot of kinky things and thought this was one of them. When I told her it was not a sex deal gone wrong, she looked at me, and said, 'What now? If you want sex, no problem. You name it, we will do it. I have done it all.'

"This was the first time I had ever taken a girl who wasn't the least bit intimidated by the surroundings or me.

"I lit a cigarette, and put it into her mouth. She took a puff and said. 'What the crap, Man? Tell me something. Are you a pervert or something? If you are, that's fine with me but let's get on with it. I got to get back or the girls are going to be looking for me.' I told her to take it easy and give me a minute. I reached for the two briefcases that I had taken from the barrel. I took my knife and opened them, and the two together had about $15,000 in cash. One of the cases also had a kilo of cocaine. Seeing the coke, the girl said, 'It's party time! Let's do it, old man.'

"This girl was crazy and I liked it. I could see her being an asset in the future. This was a first for me but there was something about her that intrigued me. I took the tape off of her hands and feet, and we had sex several times during the night. We started out the next morning. Two days later we arrived at my friend's house.

"Sheriff, you know I am or was a cold-blooded killer. This guy would make me look like a priest. He hates the government so bad he kills anyone who speaks well of it. There was a guy in prison who defended the guards. The guy told my friend the guards were just doing their jobs. He stuck the inmate's head into boiling grease. The man lived but he was scared for life. My friend pulled two extra years and was released. Ralph is the only man I know who is worse than my friend Henry."

I was looking at BH and thinking, here is a man who kills a young woman and takes her to a shed where he cuts her up like a beef cow and he thinks this guy is worse than him because he stuck a man's head into a grease pot?

BH called for his dog unaware the dog was sitting beside him. He loved the dog. The dog and his daughter were probably the only things he had ever cared about in his miserable life.

I asked BH if at any time he ever feared the police stopping him while he had one of his victims in his van. His reply, "No. Yu know as well as anyone cops are creatures of habit. They are repetitive in

61

nature. In Vegas, I actually spent two days and nights following two cops. They went to work and the first thing they did was spend an hour and a half in a café.

"They rode around all over town taking care of personal business. Things like picking up their dry cleaning and going by a garage to get their personal cars worked on for a discount or for nothing. I even watched them pick up a hooker and take her to an alley behind a warehouse where she performed oral sex on both of them. No, I don't worry about cops. They are just like me. They just get paid for what they do.

"I have one plan for cops if I get stopped and it looks like I might be going to jail. I simply shoot them. I have no reason to fear going back to jail. I have no reason to fear being put to death. I died many years ago. I just haven't been buried yet."

The more I listened to BH, the more I understood him. This man was a genius and, in an odd way, highly educated. He was articulate and well-versed in many things. He also was very laid back under any circumstance. I guessed he had faced the fact he had been born to give pain and misery to others. Or it could have been because he knew he already was at death's door.

BH took a sip of wine and asked about my family. He knew I had two sons, and he tried to get a conversation started about them. I quickly told him I never talk about my family in a working environment. He laughed and said, "I fully understand that, Sheriff."

He returned to his story.

"My friend Henry was waiting down at the gate to his ranch. You had to cross a river by a small bridge to get there. Henry's place was about a mile back in the hills. A mile beyond his place was his dad's old German siding house. We walked around to the front of Henry's Ford truck and I asked about the price for staying. He said it would be fifteen-thousand dollars including food and services. He followed me up to the house and showed me around. The place was small but perfect for my needs. After spending much of my life in a six by six cell, this place was a palace.

"After Henry left, I pulled the girl out of the van and took her inside. Henry had thought of everything -- booze, food and a radio. I never watched much TV but Henry had a small one in the kitchen.

"I removed all the tape and told her to go take a shower. I went to the kitchen and poured a drink and took my clothes off. I then got into the shower with the girl. As the water ran down her face I placed my hand around her neck. She showed no fear. She took a bar of soap and started washing my back while putting her face down on my chest.

"I pushed her back against the shower and tightened my grip on her neck. She never resisted. A washcloth had fallen on the floor and blocked the water from draining out. She started bending down and I released my grip. When she bent over to pick up the cloth, I moved behind her. We had sex and when she didn't resist, I knew I would keep her around for my desires."

The detail that BH used in his stories was unbelievable. He wanted your attention and knew exactly how to get it. It was apparent he either had a photographic memory or was the best liar I had ever run across. He continued his story.

"The girl and I got along great. We just had sex and did cocaine every day. She told me that she was from a small town in Tennessee and had been molested by her brother and father. Her mother died in a car wreck and her dad and brother took the insurance money and opened up a small mowing business. Both of them got hooked on crack cocaine and would rape her three or four times a week.

"They wouldn't allow her to have friends and made her quit school to cook and clean for them. They told her she was nothing but a whore and they would kill her if she told anyone about what they were doing to her. One night while they were asleep, she stole their truck and went to Kentucky. From there, she hopped a bus to Vegas. She had a thousand dollars she had stolen from her brother's wallet.

"When she stepped off the bus in Vegas, Momma Pimp, the big black lady I had left at the shop, approached her. Momma Pimp got her a room and told her she would take care of her.

"Within a few days, she was doing cheap tricks, oral sex and private dancing for bachelor parties. Once she was sent to a party at a private residence just outside of Vegas where a Chinese wanted kinky sex. When he started getting too rough, she tried to leave and he repeatedly raped her. After he had fallen asleep, she got a large knife from the kitchen and returned to the bedroom. She plunged the knife into his throat and stabbed him twenty-five times in the chest.

"She told Momma Pimp what had happened, and Momma Pimp put her up at her house for a month. The man's body wasn't found for two months and the girl never heard any more about it.

"Now I knew I would keep her for a while. She too, had tasted blood and liked it.

"We spent three months in the house and I finally decided to take a trip into town. It was a small tourist town located just north of the Northern Gate of Yellowstone Park. I bound the girl and told her I would be back in an hour or so. She was okay with being bound; she knew why I had to do it. I didn't tape her mouth and placed her in front of the little TV.

"I took the van and went into town and made a call to Ralph. We had developed a code in which we would use certain words with numbers. This enabled us to communicate even if someone was standing by the phone. I told him where I was located and let him know I would be heading his way in a few days. I stopped by the little store located five miles from the house and picked up some beer and supplies.

"When I returned to the house, I noticed Henry's truck parked out back near the barn. I knew him and he would be there for only one reason -- looking to steal something. I stuck my pistol into my belt and headed for the side window of the house. When I looked in, I could see Henry. He had her on the bed and was doing her. He was hitting her on the backside and talking to her. I couldn't make out the words but I could imagine what he was saying.

"I walked around to the back door and slowly turned the knob. Once inside, I put my back to the wall. Henry spoke to the girl, 'Move it baby, move it. If you don't, I'm going to get rough and you won't like it.' The girl wasn't saying anything but I could hear grunting and moaning. She was tough and this was nothing new to her.

"I slid the pistol from my belt and quietly pulled the hammer back. In order to bring down that big son-of-a-bitch, I would have to shoot him in the knee or leg. If I shot any higher I might hit the girl. I wanted to kill him but I knew I would be no match for him man-to-man.

"I heard him spanking her behind and she was moaning louder and louder. The bed was rocking back and forth with the headboard hitting the wall. The banging was so hard it knocked two pictures off of the wall. I eased down on the floor rested on my knees. He was yelling obscenities at her.

"I slid forward and aimed for his right knee. I squeezed off a round from the .357 Magnum. It struck him just below the knee and sent him to the floor with his pants down to his ankles. He fell to his side. Blood and bone could be seen on the green rocking chair a few feet away. As I went through the door, I noticed his shotgun against the wall near the bed. He yelled out, 'I will kill you, you jerk!'"

"The girl had rolled off the bed and landed on a red rug with green borders.

"I pulled her up and removed the tape from her ankles. She pushed her hair back and yelled, 'Kill him. BH, Kill that son-of-a-bitch!' I told her to get the shotgun and hold it on him. Henry crawled over and rested his back on the wall.

"Henry was bleeding pretty badly and breathing hard. He looked up at me. 'Why in hell would you shoot me over that whore?

She is just a slut, common white trash,' he said. Before I could answer I heard a large BOOM! It was so loud in my ear I went down on one knee. It caught me off guard and I couldn't hear a damn thing. I looked back toward the girl, and she was standing there with the shotgun in her hand with the smoke flowing out of the barrel. The smell of gunpowder filled the entire house.

"She walked over to Henry and put the barrel to his head, or what was left of it, and said, 'Here is your whore; how do you like her now?' Henry somehow was still alive. He was trying to say something but I couldn't understand him. The girl reached over and took my pistol and shot him in the crotch. She handed me the pistol and went into the kitchen, picked up a bottle of bourbon, and took a drink.

"I walked over and gave her a big kiss. 'Good girl,' I said. Henry was still breathing; so I walked over and put a bullet in his temple. Now he was gone, and we needed to start packing and heading out.

"Before we reached the van, I turned to the girl and asked, 'What is your name? ' She put her right hand on my face and said, 'You want the real one or the one I like to use?' I grabbed the side door of the van and said, 'Doesn't matter to me, girl.' She told me, 'Cherokee is what I go by. My grandmother was full-blooded Indian.'

"I laughed, and said, 'Okay, I will just call you Squaw.'

"We left and headed east toward New York. That's where I wanted to meet Ralph and make arrangement to find a house. With the money I had, I could get a decent house for a change.

"Ralph had a house waiting for us by the time we arrived in New York. I gave him ten-thousand dollars and told him to find me a different van. I wanted a bigger one with a bath and larger bed. In New York you can get anything you want from the underground market. Cars, tags, driver license, registration cards, you name it.

"Ralph took Cherokee out and bought her new clothes from the garment district warehouses. Most of them probably were stolen from the docks or were knockoffs from the fine ladies clothes.

"I had to pay off some drug bills to the boys down near the

docks. I took Cherokee with me and she really enjoyed the thug life. I had to control her some of the time because she had a foul mouth and didn't realize how bad these guys were. It wasn't they were tougher than Ralph and me; it was simply because there were a lot more of them. They never slept and if you owed them money, you had better pay up.

"Between paying for the house and the drug bill, it was time for me to go back to work. We let Cherokee go back to the streets. Ralph was her pimp and I stood by for the robbery. There was no sex, she set them up and pulled them into an alley. Then Ralph and I took down the johns.

"Ralph found a nice van with all the trimmings including a large bed and bath. It was a big step-up and because it looked like something an old retired couple would drive, it would draw less attention than the old one. Ralph had the old one crushed by a friend who ran the crusher at a large junkyard across the river.

"Everything was going well and Cherokee was turning out to be quite the little thug. With her street experience, she drew a lot of high scale johns. They all had lost money. Some even went to the ATM and withdrew cash. We stayed in New York for nearly a year until Ralph had a hunch it was time to go. That's all I needed. We headed down to Norfolk."

It was getting late afternoon and due to the damp air, BH wanted to go back up to the big house and get something to eat and take a break. I, myself, was ready for a break. I spotted the dog down near the guesthouse and went down to have a drink. I really didn't want to spend another night in that house but it looked like I was going to. After the drink, I walked over to the big house and met Ralph and BH in the smoke room.

Earlier Ralph had taken some cigars and rolled them in old brandy. He had them waiting when we went into the room.

BH then resumed his story.

"Ralph drove the van while Cherokee and I had sex and snorted the remainder of the cocaine. We would rest a while and have sex in as many ways as we could. She was sexy and great in bed. We were in bed and getting ready to light a cigarette when she had a question. 'BH, don't you want to know how old I am?' I handed her the smoke. 'Not really, baby. It doesn't matter to me.' She never asked how old I was.

"We rented a place at the beach and it was low key. Cherokee loved it and now I trusted her enough to leave her alone. She spent most her time on the beach while Ralph and I cased the area. As always, we had prison contacts but we had to be careful not to get a talker to help us. Usually, the bigger the crime they had committed, the higher you could place them up on the ladder of trust.

"It was on a weekend and we all decided to finish off the rest of the cocaine. We started about three in the afternoon and then went down to the beach. There we drank bourbon until dark.

"Ralph, who never talked about sex, asked Cherokee if she could find him a girl. He wanted a hooker, someone he could simply pay and forget about it. Cherokee took the van and returned with a white girl. She was a bleached blond with big breasts who looked to be in her late twenties. Her waist was slim, and she looked nice in shorts and a beach top.

"It was dark when we got back to the house, and Ralph wasted no time taking care of his desires. They went upstairs and you could hear them getting it on. Cherokee was super high and was getting horny herself. We didn't even go to the bedroom. She just stripped down right there in the living room. Then she walked over to the radio and found an oldies channel. The song playing was, "Stand by Me." I took my clothes off and sat on the couch. Cherokee started dancing slowly across the room. She danced over to the bathroom and came out with a bottle of sun tan oil. As she moved toward me, she put the oil all over her body. With each step she would move closer. By the time she reached the couch, she was covered and her breasts were shining from the light overhead.

"When she reached the center of the room, she got down on her hands and knees and started growling like a tiger. She climbed on the couch and started rubbing me down with the oil. She sat on top of me and was squirting that stuff all over me when we heard a loud scream from upstairs. I threw Cherokee off and ran up to see what was going on.

"When I reached the top of the stairs, the hooker was climbing on all fours toward me. She was naked and screaming, 'He's crazy, he's crazy, he tried to choke me to death!' Ralph was standing outside the door and his large body cast a shadow against the wall behind him. He had his belt in his hand and was sweating like a whore in church.

"Like me, Ralph was crazy and I didn't want any physical confrontation with him over a hooker. He told me the girl promised to do anything he wanted but when he started choking her with the belt, she kicked him in the crotch and jumped out of the bed.

"I told Ralph and the girl to follow me downstairs; we were all naked as a jaybird standing in the middle of the large room. Once Cherokee found out what had happened, she went off on the hooker. 'Hey bitch, you got in this business for the money,' Cherokee said. "I explained everything to you before you came here. I should take that belt and choke you myself. Now get your stuff and get in the van.'

"I knew then we would have to leave the house and move on. Things like this are not good. The girl might go back and tell her pimp what had happened and he would bring some guys looking for us. We would get into some heavy stuff and the next thing you know, the cops would be after us.

"I told Cherokee to give the girl an extra two-hundred dollars. Within two hours we were on the road. Ralph drove while Cherokee and I snorted the last of the coke. Ralph had a friend near Culpeper, Virginia, but I told him we would just find a cheap campground and set up there for a few days. I liked the idea there's not much business in a small town. We would just chill for a couple of days. We needed drugs but didn't want to deal with small town dealers; they talk too much and have bad stuff.

"Cherokee was starting to get the shakes from the lack of drugs so we headed deeper south."

Chapter Eight

Cherokee the Thug

"We went to Atlanta after a quick stop in North Carolina. We stopped off in Charlotte and visited a meth dealer I knew but had to wait a few hours while he got some good stuff. Meth is a lot worse drug but we had to have something before we went into withdrawals

"After getting about 10 miles outside of Atlanta, we put the camper into a spot, which belonged to an old man and woman. The place was perfect because we were the only camper in the place. The owners were going to Florida and asked if we would pay up front. We had the whole place to ourselves.

"We spent the next three weeks finding scores in Atlanta but the money was giving out and nothing was coming in. We knew we had to put Cherokee back to work.

"Atlanta is a tough place. Unlike New York, it isn't large; therefore, it has smaller gangs which have a smaller area to cover. They can concentrate on tinier portions of the city. Regardless of how small the competition may be, pimps take it very seriously when you move in on their territory.

"We would be rogues and would really have to protect Cherokee from being killed. For the average citizen who hears about prostitutes and pimps, they can only picture images from movies or TV. Many depict them as being in a 'cool' or sometimes funny business. Believe me, these people will kill anyone who tries to take over even a small amount of their business.

"Ralph and I parked the van across the street from hot spots in town and watched as Cherokee made her rounds in and out of the clubs. She was hot and sexy and it was only a matter of time before she started making contacts.

"She knew how to feel out the men and learn about their incomes and maybe get information about their families. We didn't want any young studs who were single and just looking for a good time. Middle age men and older were her marks.

"The more they had to lose, the more she would tease them. The plan was only to be seen for the first three nights. On the fourth night and beyond, it became a bidding war among the old rich guys. No all-night motel romps; it would be just a quickie in the back of his Mercedes or BMW. This gave us control of the situation and it would be over in five minutes.

"Cherokee always asked to see the cash while still in the club, and she only agreed to a deal when the money was substantial. Most wealthy guys only used credit cards but if they were swingers and dealmakers, they knew cash always has been king.

"We parked in the back of the parking lot where we had a good view of the whole place. The biggest problem we usually had with the rich guys was valet parking. Cherokee knew how to get around that by enticing the john to walk her to the car and it worked every time.

"When they came out, Ralph and I could see the guy was usually at least in his sixties. I remember that one of the guys stopped and lit a smoke and fixed his shoe. He was a very short man who was dressed in a very expensive dark suit and tie.

"As soon as they crossed the street and tipped the parking lot attendant, Cherokee stopped and gave the man a long kiss. This was going to be a big score. The kiss was a typical signal to us. If it were a good score, Cherokee would light a cigarette and take one puff and throw it away. If it were a super score, she would take three puffs.

If she stopped and kissed the john, this meant he had some bigger cash in his home or office. Many of these rich guys had condos or houses hidden from their wives. This is where they took hookers or girlfriends. Cherokee knew we didn't want to go to a place where there were other people or cameras.

"After she kissed the short man, he started fondling her and rubbing her rear. We knew he was hooked. We could see her talking to him and pointing to the opposite end of the parking lot. We had used this before. She was telling him she had to go pee and couldn't wait any longer. Ralph got out of the van and made his way to the other end of the lot and hid behind a car.

"Cherokee went over and squatted behind a car. Ralph was behind the car next to her. She told Ralph the man said he had a house on the outskirts of town and wanted her to spend the night for two-thousand dollars. She told us to follow them in the van, and she would make sure the man drove slowly enough for us to keep up. He was a retired investment banker and was married. When she returned to his vehicle, she got behind the wheel. Cherokee was a natural thug.

"We made it to the john's house around midnight. The place wasn't what we expected. The small house was not in one of those gated communities with security guards riding through ever hour or so. It did have a gate, but it was small and it sat alone.

"When they pulled up to the gate, Ralph dropped me off and I ran to the ivy-covered fence. I quickly climbed the fence and waited on the other side for Ralph to join me. I knew the old man had to give Cherokee the code to open the gate so we would have the code when we left.

"Sheriff, I know you understand about the 'Rush Factor,' but most everyday working stiffs or average housewives don't have a clue why people like me will always be the same. While standing there against the fence and watching the car pull up into the drive, I got goose bumps and my hair stood up on the back of my neck. I was aroused sexually just at the thought of what might happen inside that house. What a wonderful feeling! It wasn't about the money. As I said before, it's about the power and control over the victim. Sheriff, do you know how hard it is to climb a fence when you are sexually aroused?" he said as he reached for the wine."

I took a bite of my liver pudding and said "No, BH. No, I don't."

His ability to tell the story in such detail continued to blow my mind. It was as though he had written it all down and memorized it. He was enjoying himself, and now I knew Ralph was actually the one I should be worried about. BH, in his weak condition, would be no match for me. Ralph would be called the Ghost if I were writing a novel. He was cold-hearted and show no emotions. I felt sure BH was aware he had implicated Ralph in a lot of crimes. I also knew Ralph was aware of it, too. This was the first time I realized a potential problem I might have with Ralph. Yet, I had given my word and was going to see it through. If I were honest, I'd admit it also took me back to something I loved to do. I love to do interviews in criminal cases, and I have the ability to take the findings and fill-in the blanks and solve a case, regardless of what the case involves. I was self-indulging in skills I was known for. Of course, I don't do interviews anymore.

Damn! Now both of these guys were getting in my head. I would never have listened to anyone talk this much. However, I had never had anyone who had been able to drag me into his world. I was simply fascinated with both of these people.

I was questioning myself concerning the complexity of the three people involved in these bazaar tales of death, torture and--in a strange way--sadness. Could it be I actually understood their reasons for their actions? Could it be, based on events in my life concerning deaths I had caused in war and public service, I was questioning those situations in my life? In reality, killing someone is killing someone no matter the situation. You still have caused a life to no longer exist. You still have a mother and father without a child or a family without a son or a father. You still have left families with a lifetime of pain and suffering.

I was beginning to feel as if I had become one of the gang, while at the same time I wanted to take BH's pistol and shoot both of them. Then I would take their bodies to the nearby swamp and feed them to the alligators. I needed a break.

I headed back to the guesthouse to use the bathroom and get a cold glass of sweet tea. The old dog followed me into the house and took a seat beside the fireplace. I laid the recliner back and in a short time I was out. Dreamland started to make its way into my head. I was back in Vietnam looking down at a young Vietnamese kid I had just shot while on a night operation. He had been within the wire which protected our small perimeter surrounding our fighting position. He couldn't have been more than fifteen or sixteen.

The reflection of my face could be seen in his dark brown, lifeless eyes as they stared up at me. His skin was smooth as the black silk pajamas he was wearing. I pulled him out of the wire and placed him under a tree. I didn't want him to stay out in the hundred-degree weather. As required, I checked him for documents which might aid us in our efforts to locate the enemy.

He had a small handmade wallet in a pocket on the inside of his military vest. The only thing in the wallet was a single picture of a middle-aged man and woman with a young girl by their side. "His family, I bet," I muttered aloud. This young body lay before me in a land 14,000 miles from my home in North Carolina. I knew nothing about him; I knew nothing about the country that I was in. The only thing we two had in common was he had been trying to kill me, while I had been trying to kill him. Though it has been more than forty years, I can still see the kid's face. I was all of nineteen years old at the time.

As the dream continued, I saw the faces of dozens of people involved in murder cases I had investigated. One after another, it was always the same--silent eyes looking up for one last time reflecting my image back at me.

The dream continued with Ralph, BH, Cherokee, and me on a dirt road surrounded by a field of daisies blowing in the wind behind us. The trunk of a blue sedan was open and BH was pulling a white man out of the trunk of the car. Ralph forced the man to the ground. His hands were bound behind him. He appeared to be in his fifties and was begging for his life.

BH walked over to me and handed me the pistol and said, "Here. You do it!" I took the pistol, looked at it, and glanced over at Ralph. Cherokee came out of the car and screamed, "Kill him. Blow his head off. Shoot him!" I paused and looked down at the man as I cocked the pistol. I walked over to the man and looked back at BH. "You sure you want to do this? " I asked.

Just as I was about to raise the pistol, I felt something wet on my face and I almost fell out of the chair. The Irish setter had jumped on me and was licking my face. My dream was over. Soaked with sweat and breathing hard, I rubbed the dog's head. "That was some kind of bad dream," I thought. Washing my face in the kitchen sink helped me get the cob webs out after that hard nap. I secured the knife around my leg and headed back to the big house. BH and Ralph were having a conversation when I walked through the door. Ralph pulled a chair out for me, and BH glanced at me and immediately went back to his story.

"Cherokee pulled the car into the garage and the door slowly moved down behind the car. Ralph and I went around to a side window of the garage. We could see Cherokee and the man enter the door. We went around to the back of the house.

"With my pen light I checked out the room. It was a child's bedroom with all the trimmings. Posters of sports people were all over the walls. I went to the next room and it was the master bedroom with a door going into a bathroom. Seeing this told me one thing for sure. This wasn't a hidden love shack. This was the old man's house. Maybe his wife and kids were away on vacation or something. Ralph looked at me and said, 'I will be right back; I forgot something in the van.'

"I walked around to the front and hid behind the shrubs located outside the dining room. The old man was mixing drinks for him and Cherokee and had removed his jacket. Cherokee was walking around the room looking at all the fancy china and glassware. The old man took her hand and led her out the door. I moved quickly and found them in a large living room. Cherokee walked over to the fireplace and gazed at a large ornate clock sitting on the mantel.

"The old man placed his drink on the mantel and surprised me by walking toward the window. I hunkered down on the ground. The light dimmed as the john lowered the window shades. I eased back up and looked back and forth through a small slit in the shade until I could see both of them.

"The old man now had his arms around Cherokee's waist. She had her drink in one hand and was using her finger to rub his lips. Cherokee knew we were outside and was allowing him to get excited. They walked over and took a seat on the white leather couch. I was concentrating on them when I felt a hand on my shoulder. It was Ralph. He held up a small camera and said, 'We'll need this.'

"Ralph went back to the garage to see if the door was unlocked He soon stepped out and gave me thumbs up. The old man was now rubbing Cherokee's legs and had laid her down on the couch. I could see Cherokee speaking to him while she rubbed his head. He stood up and removed his shirt and his belt. Within seconds, he pushed Cherokee's dress up above her waist revealing her black panties.

"I left the window and joined Ralph in the garage. As we entered the house through the kitchen, we could hear Cherokee and the old man moaning. I eased around the corner with Ralph, camera in hand, leading the way. When we reached the doorway, we could see Cherokee and the old man engaged in intercourse. He was behind her and she had her hands on the back of the couch.

"Ralph stepped out and flashed the camera and I moved around him with my pistol in a ready position. The old man was so shocked he fell backwards across a coffee table. I walked over and held the gun on him. Ralph took a picture of him on the floor, naked and breathing like a horse. He was in total shock and fear.

"Cherokee pulled off her dress and went over and sat on top of the old man. She said, 'Here, take another picture.' We let the old man up and explained the deal to him. I told him we wanted any cash and jewelry he had in the home. He could show us right now and he would be okay. If we searched the house and found anything, we would get in touch with his wife or the press and give them the camera.

"He wanted to put his clothes on but I denied the request. 'Get busy,' I said. He went to his bedroom and pulled out a briefcase and gave it to me. He said it contained roughly nine thousand dollars. He was shaking and talking to himself. A lot of people do this. It wasn't unusual for us to see this happen. It's the fear of dying and the realization of just how stupid they have been.

"He walked to a small closet and removed some things. He opened a small wall safe and handed us jewelry and a stack of stock papers. I hit him in the back of the head with the pistol and told him to leave the papers. The guy seemed to be on the verge of a heart attack and could hardly make it back to the living room. I let him put his clothes on and told him to have a seat. 'Can I have the camera now?' Before I could answer, Cherokee chimed in, 'Are you crazy, old man? You're lucky we don't blow your head off!' We left the house and headed back to the campground.

"We had a good haul from the short man's house. The diamond jewelry we got from the safe would be of no use to us if we had to hunt down a buyer. We couldn't take it to a pawnshop until we went back in Virginia."

Chapter Nine

Diamond Buyer Found

"I figured we had other business in Virginia, too. There was something I wanted to take care of there. I wanted to hunt down Cherokee's father and brother and pay my respects. The more I thought about what they had done to her, the more I wanted to set things right for her.

"We left the next morning and headed down to New Orleans where Ralph and I had connections for buying more cocaine or methamphetamine. The meth made us more paranoid and dangerous. You have no control of your emotions when you take that stuff. Whenever you hear about some nutcase who just walks into a store or restaurant and shoots everyone in broad daylight, in most cases, the shooter is using meth.

"After hearing Cherokee complain all the way down to the Crescent City, we rented a room down in the French Quarter. The meth was causing me to get careless, and Ralph wanted to distance us from the girl. Between the drugs and the sex, I was not my normal self. I was twenty years older than the girl and middle-age crazy was all over me. Although the French Quarter has a cop on every corner at night, during day you can't find one. Cops on Bourbon Street are too busy fighting drunks and hookers to worry about drugs and cash being passed around.

"Ralph brought the cash and diamonds, and the three of us headed down to Bourbon Street to look for contacts to buy the diamonds. We had to be careful because undercover agents are all over the place. Those officers aren't looking for drugs as much as they are looking for pickpockets. The French Quarter has hundreds of pickpocket artists.

"After two nights of looking, Ralph found a guy who had a shrimp boat down at the docks. He was from Central America and had the perfect cover for hauling drugs. He would meet boats ten miles out and stuff the drugs into the mouths of fish and cover them with three feet of ice. The man bought the diamonds and arranged a meeting for the next night.

"We arrived at the dock shortly after dark and were met by a dark-skinned man with a worn white captain's cap. With that cap and a long cigar, he looked like a pirate. His thick beard and thicket of gold chains around his neck made him look even more clandestine. Ralph knew the man's brother who had been, of all things, a prison guard for a while at a small prison in Florida. He had been fired from that job for sneaking smokes to the inmates.

"We ran into a problem when the captain of the boat said Cherokee couldn't go along. I offered him five hundred dollars to allow her to go but he still refused. Ralph went with the captain, and Cherokee and I waited at a bar across from the dock.

"That bar was a dive and filled mostly with older fisherman. A fat Cuban was behind the bar pouring beer while a not-so-young waitress was humping tables. Cherokee and I took a seat in a corner where the light was low. The waitress came over and took our order. She was one of those women who prompt you to say, 'I bet she was good looking in her day.' A Calypso band started playing Cajun songs and the place lit up. A few girls came in and the crowd started dancing and having a good time.

"We had several drinks, and I went out to check the docks to see if the boat had returned. A man was standing on the dock looking out to the gulf. Dressed in an old Navy pea coat, he paced slowly back and forth. Smoke swirled up from a cigarette in his left hand. As I got near him I saw him reach into his pocket. I walked up and said, 'Hey, can I get a light?' He pulled a Zippo lighter from his pocket and clicked it to give me a light. That was a sure telling sign he had been in military service, probably the Navy.

"There's nothing like the snap of a Zippo lighter and the taste of a good cigar. The man was slightly built and had a heavy voice. 'I'm waiting on Captain Rico to come in. How about you?' I really didn't know the captain's name but I said, 'My friend is out on a boat with a guy. I'm just waiting on them to return.'

"We chatted a few minutes until we heard the sound of a boat coming out of the fog. It was Ralph and he was standing behind the captain. It was like Ralph to be standing *behind* someone. He doesn't trust anyone. The boat docked and the captain threw a rope to the man in the pea coat and he tied it to the dock.

"Ralph held up his thumb as a confirmation he had the stuff and he headed my way. The captain invited us over to the bar for drinks. When we went back into the bar, I looked to the corner for Cherokee. She was not there and I quickly scanned the room for her. She wasn't to be found. Ralph, the captain, and the stranger took seats in the corner.

"Ralph shook his head when I told him I was going to look for the girl. Outside, I didn't see her anywhere. I headed down the street and passed an alley. I heard Cherokee's voice and turned back and walked down toward a white car parked near a dumpster.

"Cherokee was sitting in the front passenger's seat with her arm out the window. A person who appeared to be a man was sitting in the driver's seat. I pulled my pistol and made my way toward the driver's side of the car. When I reached the trunk, the interior light came on. It was obvious they were doing cocaine or meth.

"Cherokee placed a small mirror on the dash and wiped her nose off with her arm. The man had his left arm on the steering wheel and his right hand across the back of Cherokee's seat. I remained still and watched as he began to stroke her hair. I could hear Cherokee tell him, 'No. You shouldn't do that. I have a man and I've got to get back before he returns.'

"The man grabbed her hair. 'Look, bitch. You took my coke and now you're going to give me something in return,' he said. Cherokee tried to open the door, and the man tried to pull her down on his crotch. Cherokee reached up and grabbed the mirror and slapped him in the face. He held her head with his right hand and unzipped his pants with his left. He pulled her head down on his privates and said, 'Now, pay your bill, bitch!'

"I pulled the hammer back on the .357 Magnum, placed it against his head and said, 'and just how much is her bill?' He let go of Cherokee's head and she jumped up to see me standing there.

"BH, she said, as she fixed her hair. I looked at the guy. 'Now, asshole, you put your hands through the steering wheel and grab the dash.

"Looking at the girl, I said, 'You get your ass back to the bar and join Ralph, I will deal with you later.'

"The guy said he only was having fun and wasn't going to hurt the girl. I opened the door and told him to get out and lay down on the pavement. He lay down, and I kicked him in the face. I beat him on the back of the head with the pistol and then stabbed him in the kidneys with my pocket knife.

"He tried to roll over but I held him down with my knees. I stood up and kicked him more. He was saying, 'Stop, please stop, I'm sorry!' I rolled him over and took the knife and cut his face like cat whiskers. He screamed with pain and tried to block my thrust with the knife. His face was covered with blood. As I was walking away, I could hear him begging, 'Please don't leave me here. I have a wife and kids. Please.' By the time I reached the end of the alley, his pleas were dying out.

"I returned to the dock and used a faucet there to wash up before going back to the bar. Ralph and the guys were shooting pool. Cherokee was seated and looking into her purse. She knew I wasn't happy. She started to say something, but I stopped her. 'Just sit there and shut up,' I said, as I moved away.

"Ralph and the guys had finished talking, and we had been offered a deal for us to work with them for a while. We agreed to meet on the boat the next day and work out the details.

"The rest of the night was uneventful and Cherokee, induced with the drugs, slept through the night.

"The next morning, the three of us met the captain at the boat and headed out to sea. The stranger turned out to be the first mate of the boat and his name was Luke. Luke took over the wheel and the rest of us went below. I explained to the captain that the girl could be trusted and I would be responsible for her at all times. He had a bottle of Tequila and poured four shots.

"I was sure we were going to talk about drugs but what he proposed involved young Mexican girls, ages fifteen to eighteen years old. The captain would transport ten girls each week and bring them to the U.S. side. We would meet the boat back up river and pick up the girls. We would deliver the girls, first to a warehouse for inspection and later to a place downtown.

"Cherokee spoke up and said, 'What happens to the girls?' Ralph and I looked at her and without saying a word she knew she had spoken out of turn. You never get involved with the deal unless you are asked to do so. It was all about the money.

"Ralph nodded in agreement to the deal and we all toasted the shot glasses and took another drink. After about an hour and a half, we came upon a fishing vessel being operated by four rough looking Mexicans. The captain was a large fat man with an unkempt beard. The Mexicans wore brown uniforms covered with stains. We tied the boats together and the Mexicans came aboard. They were really nasty looking, and three of them spoke only Spanish. The captain spoke broken English and was difficult to understand.

"It took about thirty minutes for Captain Rico to finalize the deal. The Mexicans were eyeing Cherokee and talking amongst themselves. When we arrived back at the docks, Ralph and Cherokee went over to the bar while the captain and I stayed on the boat to talk about cash. I told him I had been around long enough to know he was padding the price in his favor, and he should agree that each of would take $4,000. He laughed and agreed quickly. I knew he was probably getting around $25,000 for the deal.

"After the girls were picked up, we were to take them inside the warehouse and meet some Chinese guys to make the exchange. If we were asked to make deliveries to another location, it would require extra payment. It would be all ours. Captains Rico's involvement stopped at the dock.

"When we returned to the bar, there was a police car parked down near the alley. No blue lights, just flashers. I took a quick glance and went inside. Ralph was at the bar and Cherokee was at the table. Ralph motioned for me to follow him out back to the open beer garden. He told me a cop had come into the bar and asked questions about a man who had been stabbed in the alley last night. The incident was reported when the victim showed up at the hospital. Ralph and I agreed the man probably couldn't identify Cherokee or me. If so, the cop would have questioned Cherokee right off."

Having been a sheriff, I understood what BH was talking about. He was wise about how law enforcement situations worked. If you couldn't identify people involved in a case, you couldn't make an arrest. It was as simple as that.

Cases like this weren't uncommon. People who live double lives are often the subjects of crime. They are in places doing things they aren't suspected of doing. They may be a banker during the day and a drug user or hooker hunter by night. I was sure the man BH had attacked probably told the old story about going into an alley to take a leak and was robbed by a crackhead. He didn't remember anything.

I have taken statements from victims while they are alone, and I have taken them while their wife was sitting beside them. Believe me, you often get a different story when the wife is listening.

People like BH and Ralph know victims have placed themselves in a no-win situation and most often will not tell the truth to the police or family. What is a man going to say in front of his wife or girlfriend? "Honey, I was doing some cocaine with a hooker in a dark alley while I forced her face down in my crotch while I was thinking how much I loved you." No. Story number one is always the one they use.

BH stood up and stretched and reached for a smoke. He looked at the dog and sat back down, and continued his confession story.

"Captain Rico made arrangements for us to park our van down at the marina at a storage area where he leased spaces for boats and other vehicles. He wanted people to get accustomed to seeing it parked there. He had banners printed to put on each side of the van, 'Fresh Seafood Delivery.'

"The day of our first pickup, we all sat around in the camper and started doing coke. Ralph wanted a girl but Rico was against bringing one near the van or boat. He gave Ralph and Cherokee an address and told them to go there.

"I stayed back and did cocaine and drank Jack Daniels. It was kind of nice to just sit in the van and smoke a fine Cuban cigar without interruption. Just as I lit the cigar, there was a knock on the door. Rico came in and did a line of coke and poured a large drink of whiskey. I noticed a large scar on his neck. It was wide and looked as though he should be in the grave. He had killer eyes, and I knew I was messing with a real bad dude. Mexicans are a family oriented group. They work in groups and if one gets into trouble and needs protection or payback, they will find the one who created the trouble and get revenge.

"I dealt with them in prison. The Mexicans and the Chinese bide their time but get you in the end. He rubbed his neck and told me that the big scar came from a fight over a woman in a Mexican bar. His brother sewed up his neck with over a hundred stitches.

"After an hour of snorting coke, the captain and I were pretty much wasted, and he finally got to the reason he had stopped by. First, he wanted to know if he could have Cherokee over on his boat for the night. He said I could have one of the young girls for a tradeoff.

"People like Rico and me know the rules when it comes to women. He also knew I was just as much of a scumbag as he was and everything at some point will have its price.

"I knew he was right but not now. He also told me, 'You know, my friend, at some point, the girl is going to get in the way. The Chinese are ruthless and we must have their trust. They have too many friends.'

"I fully understood and knew the captain was right. I felt like I had stepped in cow shit and walked into Sunday school. Every one smelled it but knew they didn't want to be the first to say something.

"Captain Rico explained that the girls we were dealing with are dispatched all over the United States. Their parents are so desperate to get them to America they will pay thousands of dollars to get them here.

"Many are from Vietnam and come here regardless of what they have to do. Any life they have here is a better life than what they have back home. A great many of them become hookers for the pleasure of rich, sick businessmen. Of course, they call them housemaids. The good looking girls go to the highest bidder and the others usually end up hooked on drugs and working for pimps in places like Vegas or New York.

"The captain said he had contacts with most of the big traffickers, and he could help us if we showed we could get the job done. Hundreds of thousands of dollars could be made. We would have to split up and run three vehicles to locations all over the country. Rico said he would furnish the vans and traveling cash.

"Cherokee returned and said she had a girl for Ralph, and she was in a motel up the street. Captain Rico gave us instructions for the pickup that night at the marina.

"Ralph finally showed up around midnight. We pulled the van to the marina dock and waited for the boat to arrive. In a few minutes, Captain Rico arrived in with the boat.

"The captain gave me directions to the warehouse which was up the river, and he headed out with the girls. Following the directions, it took us about an hour to reach the place where we were to meet the captain. The road ran along the river with the warehouse sitting about two hundred yards from the road. A nightlight gave us a view of the parking lot. We could see a pier in the background. Three Mercedes cars were parked near a large garage door toward the river.

"Ralph and I stuck our pistols into our belts as we slowly drove the van down to the warehouse. We waited for nearly an hour before we heard the engines of what we hoped was the captain's boat.

"After the boat was docked, Captain Rico met us. We sent Cherokee over to the boat where the girls were locked down below. Our knock on the warehouse door was answered by a huge Chinese man in a Hawaiian shirt. He looked to be around six feet ten and close to three hundred pounds. He never spoke a word as he guided us down a maze of hallways. Finally, we reached the main floor of the warehouse. Parked in the middle of the garage was a large box truck with a furniture company logo on the side.

"Three small Chinese men and a woman emerged from an office door and approached the captain. The captain spoke a few words and motioned for Ralph and me to follow him. We went to the boat and herded the girls to the warehouse.

"The Chinese woman walked around the girls several times, and then told them to undress. The naked girls were inspected again. This time the Chinese woman put on latex gloves and did a cavity search on each of the girls.

"The captain spoke to the man with a briefcase, and in a few minutes we were told to take two of the girls and put them into the van. We loaded them up and the captain gave us an envelope with eight thousand dollars and a map. The map showed a place where we were to take the girls. It was about a 30-minute ride up the road.

"One girl was Asian and the other was Mexican. Both were very pretty and dressed poorly. Cherokee gave them some cookies and soft drinks as we made our way up the road. To my surprise, Cherokee started speaking Spanish with the Mexican girl. I never knew she could speak the language.

"We arrived at a small house on a dead end street. Following the instructions, we pulled into a side driveway. Two Chinese women came out, gave Ralph another envelope and took the girls inside. Ralph opened the envelope and pulled out two thousand dollars. Not bad for a thirty minute drive.

"As the weeks passed, we were rolling in cash but we were also spending a lot of money. Drug use by Cherokee and Ralph had increased, and I was doing meth every day. Most of our cash was going into our habit. Within a month, we were moving twenty girls a week.

"Captain Rico was taking several beat cops on fishing trips and, of course, none of them paid a dime. The lawmen also drank with the captain at certain bars. Because the captain was known for selling fish throughout the city, the van with his sign on it didn't cause suspicion by the police. We were able to deliver girls without any problem.

"We really had a good deal going and the Chinese began trusting us more. They trusted us so much that they no longer required Captain Rico to be present when we made the deals. The big bodyguard no longer accompanied the other people with the box truck.

"Cherokee wanted to move into a house or apartment, so we found a place a mile and a half from the warehouse. Ralph had a steady hooker and spent a lot of time in hotels. With her part of the money, Cherokee became more independent and we fought often. Between all the drugs used and the stress of the business, we were becoming more and more paranoid about each other.

BH stood up and said, "Sheriff, it's time for a cigar and brandy." We headed toward the house, and Ralph rolled BH's wheelchair toward the back entrance to the cellar and piano room. Ralph had a small table waiting with the brandy and cigars in a wooden tray.

Ralph walked onto the old stage and starting playing softly on the piano. Although he played lightly, the tunes were lively ragtime blues.

"I just love New Orleans and its music. How about you, Sheriff?" Ralph asked, as he took a drink of brandy.

I lowered my cigar and replied, "Yes. I like it too. I've been there on Bourbon Street several times. I was over there once when I was a soldier. Some of my fellow recruits and I had to spend the night in the old YMCA. One of them was a Cherokee Indian from Oklahoma. He got into a fight in a bar across the street from the Y. The fight came out into the street and the rest of us got involved and the police came. Being soldiers, they were gracious and let us go. So, yes, I love the music, especially the street performers."

The talking stopped, and Ralph continued playing BH's favorite songs. Even as a novice of the arts, I was impressed with Ralph as he swayed back and forth at the piano. I continued to be blown away by these two monsters. God only knows all of the horrible things they have done.

Ralph's fingers flew lightly across the piano keys, and BH continued his story:

"It was a Friday night, and a storm was coming into New

Orleans. Captain Rico was out on the water bringing more girls for our business. Our group was waiting for him in the van.

"As the rain hit the marina, the boats docked there began to bump against the piers. We could hear the bumping sounds as the camper rocked in the storm. The three of us were wasted from the drugs when Cherokee brought up the idea of robbing the Chinese. She said nobody was likely to contact the cops. Captain Rico would never contact them because he would fear being indicted. We could head back to New York and lay low and have enough cash for years. We could even leave the country, Cherokee said.

"The storm had increased and Ralph decided to go down to the dock and see if the boat had arrived. I did another line of coke and left the camper to join him. We were there for only a few minutes when we heard the boat and saw it's flashing lights approaching.

"Captain Rico docked the boat and started to unload the girls. All six girls were Mexicans, and all of them were seasick. They were throwing up and one girl was crying.

"We loaded the girls into the van and drove to the warehouse. The rain was getting worse when we pulled into the parking lot. Those Mercedes were sitting in the lot. Someone was backing the box truck inside the warehouse. Ralph and Cherokee pulled out their pistols and checked them for loads. The drugs were ruining our minds, and I knew what we were about to do was crazy.

"We took the girls in the normal way and lined them up near the box truck. The Chinese lady had two men with her. The men stood by the box truck as the woman made her usual inspection of the girls. Cherokee made her way to the men and asked them for a light. Ralph walked to the end of the line of girls which placed him close to the second man. I stood a few feet away.

"While the lady was conducting the cavity search, I walked up and put my pistol to the back of her head. I yelled, 'Nobody moves'. As soon as the words left my mouth, the woman jumped up and started kicking me. Cherokee pulled out her pistol and shot the guy in front of her right in the face. The second man tried to draw his pistol but Ralph shot him in the side of the head. As he fell to the floor, he fired one shot from his automatic pistol. The Mexican girls, still naked, ran to the back of the box truck and squatted down.

"The Chinese woman pulled a small knife and cut me on the stomach. I grabbed her by the arm, swung her around, and shot her in the chest. She ran a few steps and fell to the floor. Cherokee shot the woman three times in the head and kicked her.

"A large fan located in the far gable of the building was drawing out smoke from all the gunfire. Damn. Everything went south in a hurry and now we were left with the six girls and a mess to clean up. Blood was all over the floor and was running toward a drain in the floor under the box truck.

"Ralph walked over to me and asked what we were going to do with the girls. Before I could answer, I heard, 'Boom, boom, boom, boom, and boom!' There was silence, then another 'Boom!'

"Cherokee had shot all the girls. She reloaded and shot them again and said, 'That's what we do with the bitches! Let's check the truck and get the hell out of here.'

"Ralph gave me a wink and moved to the truck. We found a briefcase loaded with two hundred and fifty thousand dollars in one hundred dollar bills. Cherokee went nuts and started dancing around the big truck. Ralph checked the cab of the truck and found two kilos of cocaine and a MP-5 SK machine gun. We left the bodies and headed out."

Chapter Ten

Next Stop: Nuevo Leon

"Before we left those bodies strewn about the warehouse, Ralph put duct tape on my cut.

"The only person who knew us was Rico, and we figured he would cover his own butt. The Chinese would be after him in a few hours. We always had a set time to return to the marina. If we failed to report by a certain time, Rico would go into hiding. We really didn't care about his fate. He was on his own.

"Instead of going to New York, we decided to head towards San Antonio, Texas. The town of Nuevo Leon, Mexico, was our destination. It was located in the northeastern part of the country on the gulf near the coast. Ralph wanted to get a boat and sell fish. We knew the first thing we had to do was to find someone who could get us across the border.

"Cherokee wanted to be near the ocean; she had liked the area where we had been around the marina.

"It took us two weeks to find a contact to get us across the border. We shelled out twenty-five thousand dollars for the passports and other paperwork. We had to be careful with our cash. Ralph slipped across the border and buried the money about ten miles from the border crossing. We crossed the border in a dump truck. The Mexican driver had placed a large heavy-duty rubber container into the bed of the truck. We got inside the container and the driver covered it with sawdust that came from a plant which made OSB plywood. Our air supply was from a large hose running out of the bottom of the truck.

"We crossed the border without a problem. Ten miles into Mexico, we met another man who had a Ford king cab truck waiting for us. It was old but sounded good. The truck was sitting in an old building and when we went inside to pay for it, we were met by three Mexicans.

"We had only kept five grand on us because we knew the kind of people we were dealing with. We were on their turf and had no help or power. They told us to turn around and take the search position, something we all knew too well. They began to pat us down. The man searching Cherokee took all the liberties he wanted. He placed his hand down her jeans and then slid the other hand up under her shirt feeling her breasts. She wasn't bothered one bit.

"Cherokee, in Spanish, asked one of the Mexicans where we could purchase weapons. He soon returned with three 9mm. and two clips and three boxes of ammo. We had thrown our guns into the river shortly after the shooting at the warehouse.

"Ralph drove back to the place where he had buried the money. It took us about an hour to find it. We headed down the coast, found a small fishing town, and quickly made our way around the streets and docks. Ralph found a nice cabin style boat that slept five people. He rented the boat for three months and we used it while we scouted around for contacts.

"It wasn't long before we had several Mexican contacts, and Ralph started booking guided fishing tours. Cherokee and I found a small villa on top of a hill overlooking the coast. It was old and run down but the rent was cheap. There were two bedrooms and a nice deck with a great view. We called it, 'Poor Man's Miami.'

"Life seemed to be turning around but we could not break the drug habit and for me, as for all drug addicts, it just got worse. Ralph was high when he took some tourists out and got lost; it took him eight hours to get back. He was so high he didn't remember where he had departed from and ended up about ten miles from where he had cast off.

"Ralph took us out on the boat from time to time. Cherokee swam in the nude. We all did coke and sometime we spent the night out on the water.

"We started calling Cherokee 'Kee.' Ralph said it was easier. She didn't mind at all. She was young and wanted excitement all of the time. She started spending a lot of time down in the village at night.

"Kee was tough enough and I knew she could take care of herself. I also knew she would be stalked by young local guys and tourists. The drugs kept me down at night, and she eventually would go down to the village on her own. Ralph was against her going alone but didn't interfere.

"Ralph and I also knew the Chinese and Captain Rico. If the Chinese hadn't killed him, he would be looking for us. Ralph said we should go farther south and get rid of the girl. She was too high profile and we didn't need attention drawn toward three strangers who were living the good life.

"For the average person, two-hundred-and-fifty-thousand dollars is a lot of money. To a drug addict, it's about six months of good living. Right on course, the money was fading and the need for more drugs was rising. Kee was hanging out at the bars until dawn and I suspected she had a man or two on the side. Her money was running out, as well, and it was only a matter of time before she would start turning tricks. The Mexicans loved the white women and often would fight over them. They fought in the streets with knives and guns just like in the Old West.

"Near the end of the tourist season, many of the bars shut down and only the old and established bars remain open. One of them was on a higher scale place that catered to the rich drug dealers and landlords. The drug dealers ran the town and the docks, and anything pertaining to money. Anyone wanting to operate a business had to go through them for permits and permission to run a business.

"Ralph, who had picked up the language, made friends with one of the large landowners. He took Ralph out on his boat a couple times a week. It was a small yacht with a crew of three Hondurans. On one occasion, Ralph heard the man talking about a white woman he had met; he was going to bring her out on the boat. On the way back, the man told Ralph how good this woman was in bed. The woman he described was Kee. He told Ralph the woman claimed she was looking to buy cocaine for her two friends.

Chapter Eleven

Loose Lips Force Fast Move

"When I heard that Kee had let her mouth overload her ass, I knew it was time for us to move on. Ralph and I would make the owner of the boat an offer and make our way to Florida. We would first deal with Kee and try to clean up the mess she had made with the new boyfriend. We didn't know how much she had told him, but we knew of one sure way to make sure he didn't spread any information she may have given him.

"The guy liked Ralph so he was the one who worked out a meeting. We cleaned out the house and put the money we had left in the boat. The owner of the yacht asked Ralph to bring Cherokee out to his boat. Ralph told me about the three-man crew, so I hid in the cabin below. Cherokee knew nothing of our plan.

"When they got on our rented boat to meet the yacht, Ralph told Cherokee why I wasn't along. He told her I was up at the house and sick from the drugs.

"I could hear the engines slowing down while Ralph was telling the crew of the yacht he was pulling alongside. I could see her lover through the porthole. He was well dressed and was holding two glasses. I knew Ralph wouldn't waste time taking care of the lover. It was my job to emerge from below and take care of the crew. It had to be quick, and we had to make sure the boats stayed tied together.

"When I emerged from down below, Ralph was walking up behind Kee. She and her lover were looking at the lights several miles away. Two-crew members were busy with the ropes. As soon as Ralph saw me, he shot the lover in the back of his head. I quickly shot the two crew members who were working on their knees. One fell backwards and the other tried to run for the cabin door. I jumped from our boat and shot him in the back. The third crewman hit me in the back and knocked me down. My pistol flew from my hand, and he began choking me. Ralph kicked him off of me and shot him again.

"Cherokee starting yelling, 'BH, I was just trying to work a deal on the man. He has plenty money. There was nothing happening between us.' I walked over and slapped her in the mouth and grabbed her by the hair of her head. I pulled her over to the body of her lover.

"His brains were all over the deck. I told her to get down on her knees and give him a good-bye kiss. She begged not to have to kiss him but I stuck the pistol to her head and made her kiss the dead man. When she got up, I could see brains and blood all over her lips. Steam was coming off his head as I pulled him near the front of the boat.

"Ralph went below to check the cabin and came back with a small bag of cash. We pulled all of the bodies down into the cabin. Ralph found wrenches and unloosened the fuel lines. We set the boat on fire and headed toward the Sunshine State.

"Kee was running around the boat saying, 'BH, I know you're going to kill me so just get it over with. Ralph you do it. I don't care. I can't take it. Please do it, Ralph!'

"'Go down stairs and get some sleep,' I told her. We all needed rest. I went to the back of the boat and lit a cigar. I could see the light from the burning yacht now a mile away. The water was smooth and that gave me a little down time.

"The sound of the inboard motor soon faded away as I fell

asleep. Before I knew it, the sun was coming up in the east. I took over for Ralph while he went downstairs and caught a few Z's. The water was still calm as we made our way across the gulf with hope of an uneventful docking in Tampa. We had to time it just right in order to avoid the Coast Guard.

"Two hours passed before I went below deck and looked at Kee. She was on her side with one of her breasts exposed. I pulled out my pistol and placed one knee between her legs. She woke-up and started to get up but I pointed the pistol at her face. I waved the pistol back and forth so as to tell her 'no.' Fear filled her eyes as she rolled over on her back.

"With the barrel of the pistol, I slid her black skirt up and revealed her black French cut panties. I moved the barrel of the pistol across her lips and down her cheek. She was tense but managed to prop up on her elbow. Slowly, I moved the barrel down to her breasts, and then down her dress to her stomach.

"I could tell she was really afraid as I placed the barrel on her panties and pushed them down to her knees. She rose up so they could be moved easily. I pulled them off and let them fall on the floor. I used my pocket knife to cut her dress from bottom to top, exposing both breasts. She was covered with sweat and her breathing had increased.

"Her eyes grew larger, and I could see my reflection in them. I placed the pistol barrel against her lips. I pushed it until she opened her mouth and began sucking on it. She looked up at me and opened her mouth and started making a clicking sound, and displayed all of her sexuality. After all, she was a professional whore. She had been with hundreds of men, and I knew at this moment she was working to save her life.

"I had all intentions of blowing her head off of those pretty shoulders. Ralph wouldn't mind and probably would help me throw her overboard. She rubbed her knee against my crotch hoping for a masculine response. I got up and pulled the pistol out of her mouth. 'Get some sleep,' I said.

"When I went back on deck, Ralph pointed to lights headed our way. It could be the Coast Guard or just another fishing charter.

"The boat passed without incident, and we hurried out of there. Our next stop would be the Alabama coast near Mobile."

Chapter Twelve

Girls Scratch and Slug

"After Ralph, Kee, and I landed the boat on the Alabama coast, we found a place to stay on the eastern shore of Mobile Bay in the little town of Spanish Fort. It was filled with poor white trash folks. Run down houses with junked cars in the front yard were common. We stayed there for two months. Ralph sold the boat and got another camper. He also found a hooker he liked named Rachel. She was covered with tattoos and had long hair she had dyed dark.

"Rachel was much older than most girls found on the streets. At her age, she couldn't find any more tricks to turn. Compared to Kee, it was like parking a Ford Pinto beside a Mercedes-Benz E500.

"She sported a big set of implants and that was what had trapped Ralph. He was a boob man and she had enough for him and the rest of the football team. She was a big woman who worked out at the GYM at least two days a week. She possessed a voice that sounded like a cross between a foghorn and a tuba. Her big baby doll eyes were hazel and had probably been attention-getters when she was in her prime.

"Ralph also was getting older and like Kee and me, the drugs had eaten up most of his brains. Under normal conditions, he would never have had a woman move in with him. He was always on me to get rid of Kee. Needless to say, Kee had no use for Ralph's woman, and I had to keep them separated much of the time.

"Kee made a call to a friend back in Virginia and found out where her dad and brother were living. The hate she had for them combined with the blood she had tasted running with me made her want revenge. Revenge was something I had thought about long ago but I wasn't going to suggest it to her. We loaded the camper and headed to Virginia to find Kee's dad and brother.

"The idea of Rachel going along didn't please me, but Ralph had tolerated Kee so I kept my mouth shut. I didn't know Rachel's background but if she slept with Ralph, I knew she had to be tough and extremely kinky. Rachel didn't have a drug problem but she did like the booze. She could pour it down and a lot of it. During the ride up to Virginia, we played poker and did drugs. We took turns driving and played the radio wide open.

"Rachel had a sister who lived near Myrtle Beach, South Carolina, and she wanted to see her. This was another example of breaking our long-standing rules. Don't involve strangers in your business.

"We pulled in to a Walmart and parked the camper. Rachel and Ralph got a taxi and went to her sister's house. That was a good move but it still made me nervous. Kee and I hadn't had sex in a while so we took advantage of the time we were alone. When you do drugs like Kee and I did, your brain tells you the things you want to do but the truth is your body parts don't agree with your brain. Kee's body was still fine. When she came out of the shower, she looked like a Hustler girl. I got excited and pulled her out on the bed. She tore my t-shirt off and grabbed my belt and jerked it off and threw it on the floor. She unzipped my pants and got down on her knees.

"I closed my eyes with anticipation when out of the blue came a knock on the door. I knew it wasn't Ralph so I pushed Kee's head aside and got my pistol and placed it under the mattress above the driver's position. I left the chain on the door and barely cracked it. It was a security guard from the mall. His car was parked with the headlights shining in my eyes. I couldn't see his face but I could see that he was unarmed.

"Kee had picked up her pistol and I knew she was prepared to use it. She thought he was a regular cop. He asked, "Is everything okay, sir?" I had heard that question from cops many times. For most men it was a display of concern. To thugs like me, it was a way to get you to drop your guard. To me he was trying to get a peak in the door. If he saw something inside the camper, he could relay it to the police. They could get a search warrant if the security guard had been dependable in giving them information at other times.

"He asked if I would mind stepping outside. He wanted to show me something. I told him I needed to get my clothes on. I shut the door and grabbed my pants and belt and put my pistol behind in my belt.

"The security guard and I walked around to the back of the camper. He pointed his flashlight toward my face, and asked if I had a driver's license. 'Sure,' I said. After I gave him the license, he went to his car. Most security police don't have the capabilities to run background checks on the spot. Just in case this one did, I walked to his car while the officer was inside using his radio. He was talking to someone inside Walmart. "Everything is okay with them," he said. I knew he was bluffing. He had checked nothing.

"He asked me to follow him to the other side of the camper. Bending over on his knee, he pointed his flashlight under the camper. As he bent down to look under the camper, I pulled my pistol and pointed it at the back of his head. Still looking under the camper, he said, 'Looks like you have a small gas leak from your generator fuel line.' I slipped my pistol back into my pants. I told him I would get it fixed in the morning. He shook my hand and left.

"I thought, 'Man, you don't know how close you came to having your brains blown out.' We left the parking lot and parked in a nearby parking lot. Ralph and Rachel returned later and I flashed my lights so they could see us.

"Ralph and Rachel were arguing when they came inside the camper. Rachel was pissed because she couldn't stay longer with her sister. Ralph did some drugs and Rachel brought out a half of gallon of booze. We headed up the coast toward Virginia.

"The arguing continued and Kee joined in, and now it became an all-out war. I turned the music up and tried to drown it all out. We had just crossed the Virginia state line when I heard Rachel scream out at Kee, 'You little slut. I will kick your ass from one side of this camper to the other.' I looked in the rear view mirror and saw Kee pick up a liquor bottle and hit Rachel upside the head. The blood immediately poured down the side of Rachel's face. Rachel shook her head and grabbed Kee by the throat.

"I pulled the camper into an old country grocery store parking lot. Ralph broke them up and told them to get out of the camper and do whatever they thought was necessary.

"There was a small picnic table and shelter nearby. The girls walked over and started cussing each other. I pulled the camper alongside of them so they wouldn't be seen from the highway even though it was about 4 a.m. and there wasn't much traffic.

"Rachel yelled at Kee, 'Bring your little ass over here and I will show you what a real woman can do.' Kee took off running and kicked Rachel in the stomach. Rachel never moved; she grabbed Kee by the hair and threw her to the ground, then ran over and kicked her in the head. Rachel pulled Kee up by the hair, and said, 'You skinny bitch, you think you can kick my ass? I'm going to show you what an ass kicking is all about.'

"Ralph went inside and got us a cigar, and we stood there and watched the girls go at it. When Rachel pulled Kee off the ground, Kee kicked her in the knee and Rachel fell to the ground. Kee then kicked her in the face. 'You big overgrown cow, you don't scare me. I will kill you, bitch,' Kee said.

"Blood was running down Rachel's face and shirt. Kee ran over to a large trash can and grabbed the metal lid and rammed the lid into Rachel's face. As Rachel fell backwards she grabbed Kee's shirt and tore it off, exposing Kee's breasts.

"Ralph looked at me and smiled. Kee's face also was bleeding, and the blood was running between her breasts and down to her navel. I was starting to get turned on and wanted her. Kee stood over Rachel and continued to hit her with the lid and yell, 'Now bitch, do you like that? You like it don't you? Tell me, bitch, do you like it?'

"Rachel stood up and grabbed Kee and forced her back toward the table. Rachel then grabbed Kee's hair and pulled her down and rammed her injured knee into Kee's face. Kee's nose started bleeding and she couldn't see because of the blood in her eyes. Kee's breasts were covered with blood and I was getting aroused. Ralph moved closer to the action as the girls started rolling around on the ground.

"They rolled down a small incline and Kee came up on top. With both hands, she pulled Rachel's top off showing both of her massive breasts. Both girls were still bleeding and it was obvious these two women were tough. The fight, even though both girls were tired, could have gone on until daylight.

"I walked over and told both girls to get up. They struggled to stand up and when they did, they were a mess. I was so aroused; I wanted to do both women at the same time. I took Kee inside and did her until the morning sun came through the windows of the camper. When I got up and prepared to head out, I could see Ralph and Rachel naked and covered with blood on the fold out bed in front.

"We headed north to find a campground near where Kee's dad and brother were supposed to be living. Again I looked in the rear view mirror and saw the naked carnage behind me. I realized how sick and demented we all were.

"The fight, blood, and sex brought back the memories of the night I had killed the woman and cut her up. I wanted to do it again but to a stranger...a young girl...maybe a college girl or even a high school girl. Just the thought of it was getting me aroused. The camper bounced along the Virginia highway. I wanted to get up the road faster and take care of the old man and Kee's brother so I could get on with finding me a girl."

Sitting there listening to this nutcase, I could only imagine how many thousands of freaks like him are roaming the highways and motel parking lots of America. I was known as a tough and sometimes overbearing lawman but you have to be that way at times to handle some of the nut cases. People thought I was trying to draw attention to myself and they either loved me or hated me. I deserved all the criticism but if all those whiners and complainers would have understood how sick the world we live in is, they would never have slept in their warm beds at night.

Ralph touched me on the shoulder and said that a nurse was coming over today to give BH his shots. We went back to the big house and an older woman was in the living room waiting on BH.

"Come with me, Sheriff," Ralph said as he opened the door. We went outside and walked about a hundred yards to a large building. Inside was an old camper. Ralph opened the door and asked me to join him inside. The only light came from the natural light coming through a large window on the side of the building. I could see dust particles floating in the stale air inside.

Ralph left the camper door open and took a seat and I did the same. As he started speaking, I was thinking of my Ka-bar knife strapped to my leg. "Sheriff, this is the camper we used on our last trip across the United States. As you now know, we were and still are two sick human beings. If BH weren't sick, we probably would still be out there raping and killing the pathetic souls who call themselves wonderful citizens by day and steal, cheat, rape and molest children at night. That's the people who try to pass themselves off as upstanding citizens.

"BH and I are just messengers from the devil. You know God has his angels and the devil has his demons. The angels have their churches while we have our prisons."

Sweat was running down Ralph's face and he was tapping his index finger on the table. He had talked more in the past five minutes than he had during the past twenty-four hours. Ralph stood, reached over to a small cooler, and pulled out two beers. He popped the tops and continued.

"You see, Sheriff, BH and I first saw you on a TV show while we were in prison. It was one of those news shows. You were riding around in your cool car and kicking in doors on drug raids. All of your deputies were dressed in black military uniforms. The prisoners in the commons area clapped and yelled when the camera was on you holding drugs and cash you had seized from a raid.

"Do you know why they clapped and cheered, Sheriff?"

Ralph's voice was growing louder and louder, and I could tell he had been holding this inside for a long time. I took a long sip of beer, and said, "No, Ralph. No, I don't."

He leaned over and put his face about two inches from my nose. "They clapped because of all of us poor sick demented bastards. We finally were seeing someone who actually understood what kind of world we all were living in. The *real* world, Sheriff! The world where young boys and girls grow up without a father and have a drug addicted mother who doesn't give a damn about caring for a child after bringing it into the world. She just wants to spread her legs and get a twenty-dollar bill to buy her next crack rock. Our world has no color. The whites try to blame crime on the blacks and the blacks say that all white people are rich and spoiled sons-of-bitches.

"In prison, we knew the truth. Black people kill each other and rob and rape their own kind. They beat their women and neglect their children. Hell, I sat in prison and listened to black guys brag about how many kids they had fathered. Some said as many as 15, all by different women. They didn't care about the kids; they just loved to screw the women.

"We white guys do the same thing but the blacks are ten times worse than us. The prison is a foundation created by the government to hide us from society. Have you ever noticed how when a crime is committed, the media and all the government officials stand in front of the camera and talk about how horrible the crime was? How sad it was for the victims? All just bullshit. They don't give a damn. It's all for show.

"The first time I was incarcerated, I was 15 years old. I was a kid from a Baptist family and went to church three times a week. My dad worked two jobs while mom looked after three girls and four boys. I got in a car with some older boys and we got in trouble. All of them got probation while I caught a year in juvenile hall.

"When I came out, I had learned to pick a lock, make whiskey, and where to stab someone to bring him down so I could beat him to death. Prison is an educational system that provides poor people with an ability to survive in the rich man's world.

"The damn low-life politicians who stand on the steps of Congress are no different than the white slave owners who stood on the veranda of this old plantation a hundred and fifty years ago. They see the same poor souls working their asses off to get to a town called 'Nowhere, USA.'

"When we were robbing the banker in Atlanta, I wanted to cut someone's head off and go to the kitchen, get a spoon, crack his skull and eat his brains. Then I wanted to cut him open and hang his guts on the fancy gate out front. People like these think they are so much better than everyone else but in reality, they are the ones who are the scum of the earth.

Ralph's face had turned blood red, and I could tell he was about to lose it. I placed my hand down near my concealed knife. If he touched me in any way, I was going to stab him in the throat.

I slid my pants leg up and placed my hand on the knife. My heart was pounding. Ralph was so close I could feel his sweat hitting my cheeks. I was seeing the real man now. He was not much different, maybe even worse, than BH.

"Calm down and have a seat," I said. Without hesitation, Ralph took a drink of beer and sat down. "Sorry, Sheriff. I just lost it," he said as he took another swallow of brew.

Chapter Thirteen

❖❖❖

One Up on Manson

I realized that Ralph, the gentle giant, was anything but gentle. His musical talents and mannerisms probably fooled many innocent people across America. I was sitting in a camper which had been used to plan and carry out some of the most brutal murders one could imagine. This group made Charles Manson look like Peter Pan and Snow White.

Glancing around the camper, I saw unmade beds and imagined what strange sex acts had taken place in those beds. How many pounds of cocaine had Ralph, BH, and Cherokee consumed in this place? It was as though I were sitting in an exhibit in a house of horrors museum.

I was seriously thinking of getting into my little Geo and heading back to North Carolina. Yet, I knew the cop side of me wouldn't let me go. I had to stay and find out what I had come down here to learn. As the great commentator Paul Harvey used to say, now it was time for the rest of the story.

I was learning a lot about the mindset of these vicious criminals. This was knowledge I wish I could have had when I was working in law enforcement. However, I will never walk down that road again. In today's police world, I would never fit in. I had been removed for the same reasons I would never be accepted again. As an old man, all of this would give me something to think about while being fed in a rocker at some nursing home.

Ralph calmed down and continued.

"Sheriff, why in the hell did you come down here to see BH? I told his daughter you would never make the trip. I doubt you know the story of his daughter so I will tell you a little about her. Karen came into this world without knowing who her daddy was.

"She was conceived in the back seat of an old Ford. Her mom left her with some friends, and from there she ended up in a foster home. Ralph's uncle, the one who ran the garage, tracked her down and arranged for his sister to raise her. Karen grew up to be a nice young lady and was really smart in school. She was the first and only member of her so called family to finish college.

"Karen married a local farmer who was raised down the road about three miles from here. They never did find her mother but BH told me she died in a fire when a meth lab blew up. The girl used to watch your TV show and when BH was a guest on the show, his uncle called and told her that was her dad on TV. BH had already left your jail before she called the network trying to locate him. She didn't realize the show was live.

"The years passed and they weren't reconciled until that day BH showed up at tell us about it until after he came down with cancer."

Ralph's rambling didn't surprise me but I was glad BH's daughter had found him. I prayed she didn't know what kind of animal had helped bring her into the world. Ralph and I walked back to the house to check on BH and found him sitting on the back porch rubbing the head of the Irish setter. He glanced up as we approached. "Sheriff, Hospice is coming out tomorrow," he said. "They say I have only a few days left but I think they are wrong. Me and old Ralph are going to fight daddy cancer for a while but we better get on with my confession just in case."

BH asked Ralph to get us some sweet tea before he continued his story.

"We had to go to a drugstore and buy bandages for the girls. Both were scratched up pretty bad. Kee had one eye-swollen shut and Rachel had a large cut on her head. Kee was in the back bedroom while Rachel was on the couch up front. We rode around until we found another mom and pop campground. We spent the day resting up and coming down off the drugs. The morning came and we waited until about noon to drive around and find the address for Kee's dad and brother.

"We found the house and, as we had expected, it was a redneck shithole. There were two junked cars in the yard and two more on the street. Several pieces of the cheap vinyl siding on the house were hanging loose. An old refrigerator stood beside the door on the front porch, and garbage bags were piled nearby. Beer cans were falling from a couple of the bags. It was a typical southern redneck place where anything to do with beer is saved. They sell the cans and turn around and buy more beer.

"We pulled the camper over to the side and parked across the street from the house. In about an hour, two men came out the front door. The older man was wearing a yellow tank top and blue jeans. He took a seat in the oak lattice swing. The other guy pulled up an old bottle crate and sat down. I figured the guy sitting on the crate was Kee's brother. I could see his long curly blonde hair sticking out from under his red ball cap.

"The old man slid the garbage bags out of the way, opened the refrigerator door, and brought out with two beers. They popped the tops and began to talk and laugh. I could hear their voices but not what they were saying. Kee came up behind me and put her hands on my shoulder. 'That's them, BH, that's them,' she said. Ralph and Rachel moved to the front and looked through the windshield. "Is that the two assholes who raped Kee?' Rachel asked. Kee slid beside me. 'Yes, that's my loving daddy and brother, the ones who beat and raped me like a slave at auction.'

"What are we going to do with them, Ralph?' Rachel asked. Ralph pulled out a cigar and reached for his lighter, then said, 'Whatever the boss man wants, the boss man gets.' I took Kee to the back of the camper and asked her, 'What do you want, Baby? You tell me and it will be done."

Chapter Fourteen

Kee's Revenge

"We returned to the campground without making a move on Kee's kin. I wanted to put together a plan. We took Kee to the mall and let her shop while me. Ralph and Rachel went back and parked across the street from that house. Rachel put on some sexy shorts and a top which exposed everything but her nipples.

"When we pulled up across from the house, Ralph got out and raised the hood of the van. He unscrewed the radiator cap and released the steam. He came back inside and took a snort of coke. Ralph told Rachel, 'Go do your magic, Baby. Bring home the fish, Baby, bring home the fish.'

"Rachel, her face sporting a large Band-Aid, walked across the street and stepped up onto the porch. She asked the men if they would give her some water for the camper. She also told them her brother had a bad arm and couldn't work on the vehicle for her. After checking out her body, the men fetched a five-gallon bucket of water and followed Rachel back to the camper.

"They stood in front of the van and talked for a few minutes while Rachel was rubbing all over them by pretending to look at the engine. I stepped back into the back bedroom and closed the curtains. Ralph had left a bag of marijuana on the table along with a bottle of Jack Daniels. The guys poured the water into the overflow box, and Rachel invited them inside. Ralph offered them a drink and they took a seat.

"It wasn't long until all of them were smoking pot and drinking Jack. The dad was getting high and sitting right beside Rachel. They were laughing and Rachel was rubbing her breasts all over the old man as the younger one looked on. Ralph told the guys he was going outside to check the engine and close the hood. As soon as he stepped outside, Rachel put her hand on the old man's crotch, and I could see him placing his hand on her legs. The brother moved over and wanted some of the action. Rachel placed her hand on his crotch and was working both of them into a frenzy.

"Ralph kept his head under the hood knowing I was there to protect Rachel. I could see Ralph when he closed the hood. He reached around with his right hand and put it on his pistol. I did the same. The older man and Kee's brother quickly pushed Rachel's hand away when Ralph entered the door. Ralph pulled his pistol and yelled, 'Put your hands on the table, boys, and don't move a muscle.' The old man started to get up, but I walked up behind him and put my pistol to his head.

"Rachel got up and got a roll of duct tape and started taping their wrists together. The older man started to say something, but I hit him in the head. Rachel then taped both their mouths. The brother tried to get up and head for the door but Ralph kicked him in the face and drove one of his teeth through the tape. I pulled the old man out of the seat and told Rachel to tape his legs together while Ralph was pulling the brother across his dad to the floor. After we taped their ankles, we headed back to the mall and picked up Kee.

"Even with their mouths taped, both men tried to speak but we had heard people beg before. I knew what was going to happen to them, and now they also were aware of it. They knew it couldn't be a robbery, but it might be a debt not paid for a drug deal. I really didn't care; I knew I was going to kill both of them. It would be up to Kee what the method would be.

"My only concern was Rachel. I really didn't know anything about her but I did know she would be a witness. I also knew I would kill her in a heartbeat and rape her as well. Which act came first didn't matter.

"Ralph drove while Rachel and I drank Jack, and Kee's dad and brother rolled around on the floor. Rachel's breasts were bouncing up and down and back and forth. She was looking at me and smiling as she put the glass to her lips. I could see her tongue licking the ice in the glass. I put my hand on the back of the seat just inches from her chest. I could feel the air being moved by her bouncing breasts. I was getting so excited and I wanted to throw her down on top of the two men on the floor and do her right then.

"I knew she could see my excitement and guess what I wanted to do. The men could see it as well and were looking at each other like they now knew a true nutcase had taken them.

"We picked up Kee at the mall and when she came through the door, I could see the men looking up at her. 'I see you got the bastards,' she said as she placed her purse on the table. She walked over to her dad and said, 'You no-good bastard, I'm going to make you pay for what you did to me all those years.' She turned to her brother and kicked him in the head. 'And you! You are worse than him.'

"I looked at Kee. 'Well, Baby, what do you want to do with them?'

"'I want you to make both of those bastards suffer,' she said as she snorted a line of coke and chased it with a shot of Jack.

"I knew the location of a large tree farm just off the interstate. A guy at the gas station had told me about it. He said a large pulp wood company down in North Carolina owned it and leased it to hunters during deer season. The farm had over 10,000 acres of trees, and the land was divided into 1,000-acre tracts. There also was a fire road that was used for logging. It sounded like a perfect place to park the camper.

"We drove down the dirt road for about three miles. I was

surprised to see how well the roads on the farm were maintained. Small logging roads intersected the main road like a spider web. We took a side road and found a small maintenance shed. There was a fence around it with a chain attached to the gate. The river was only about fifty yards from where we parked the van. Ralph was a little nervous about the possibility of someone coming to the shed.

"I agreed with Ralph about the possibility of someone coming upon us at the shed. So we moved about a hundred yards down and parked in a thicket near the river. Once we were settled, all of us started doing coke and drinking booze.

"The two men were struggling, trying to break free. Kee did a line of coke and threw her head back and said, 'Oh yeah! That's what I'm talking about!' She walked over to the men on the floor and kicked each of them in the face and turned around to me. 'Get them up and sit them on the couch,' she said. While I was getting them up, I said, 'Damn, Baby, don't these guys have a name? After all, they are your dad and brother.'

"Rachel spoke up. 'Yeah, Kee, what're their names?' Kee, pouring a shot of Jack said, 'Oh yes, they have names.' She walked over to the old man and ripped the duct tape off his mouth. The old man screamed and took a deep breath. 'This is my old man. His name is Carl. Carl's the piece of crap that made me. This one here is Junior, my brother. He raped and beat me for five years.'

"Ralph walked over to Junior and pulled the tape off his mouth and slapped him in the ear. 'So you raped and beat your sister? Big man you are, we're going to see how you like it. For us prison guys, nothing like a tender little white boy,' Ralph said.

"Both men were holding their heads down and shaking. Finally, the old man said, 'Look, all of that was a long time ago and we're sorry for it, Cherokee. We're sorry for all the stuff we did.' Before Kee could answer, Ralph said, 'Oh, you are going to be real sorry, my friend. We are all going to make sure of that in a few minutes.'

"Ralph pulled Carl up and dragged him out of the camper. I cut the tape on Junior's ankles and pushed him outside. Cherokee and

Rachel followed me. I threw Ralph my knife and told him to cut the tape on Carl's ankles. I told Cherokee to go around to the back of the camper and get the jack handle from the jack.

"Then I walked Carl out to a tree and told him to put his hands and arms around the tree. Ralph brought the duct tape over and bound Carl's mouth and wrists. I reached around Carl and dropped his pants and pulled his underwear down.

"Ralph took Junior out to the tree beside of Carl. After Junior was bound. I went to the back of the camper and got four yard chairs and took them back to the tree. I sent Kee and Rachel to the camper to fetch the bottle of Jack and a bag of weed with the bong.

"Kee was sitting there bouncing her leg up and down. I looked at her and said, 'There you go, Babe. Whatever you want.' She got up from her chair, picked up the jack handle, and walked over and hit her dad in the back of the head. She pulled the tape off of his mouth, and said, 'What do you say, Carl? Are you happy to see me, Carl?' Carl was trying to jerk his hands free when Kee took a big swing and hit him in the face. The blood splattered on the tree and Carl let out a scream.

"Junior was telling Kee how sorry he was as he watched the old man being punished. Ralph walked over to Junior and stuck his cigar right on his eyelid. Junior let out a scream, and told Ralph, 'Let me loose, you son-of-a-bitch, and I will kick your ass!' Ralph laughed and said, 'That's not how it works, boy.'

"I could tell Rachel was getting super high and wanted some of the action. I looked at her and said, "Girl, what do you think?' She stood up and went into the camper and came out with a large butcher knife. She walked up the junior and stuck him in the back. 'Hell, no need to take all day. If we are going to do it, let's do it.' Junior fell to his knees and screamed out, 'Crazy bitch, I will kill you.'

"Kee picked up a rock and started knocking out Carl's teeth. Carl was trying to cuss her but started choking on his own blood. Kee hit him in the head and I could hear his skull crack from where I was standing. It was like a bunch of lions converging on a freshly killed water buffalo. Kee showed nothing but hate for her dad and brother. The drugs had all of us at a level of insanity beyond belief.

"Carl was hanging from the tree with his knees bent and his chin on his chest. The blowflies were starting to consume the blood running down his face. I had to go into the camper and do some methamphetamine. When I returned, I wanted to cut the men into pieces and throw them into the river. Meth makes you feel like a thousand spiders are crawling all over you and you're growing extra arms to swipe them off. You feel like you have a thousand eyes to help look for the spiders but you still can't find them all. You feel like you're in a house of mirrors and no matter how many you break with your fist, another mirror appears. Your fingers are cut off but they grow back as fast as they hit the floor.

"I came out of the camper in a rage and went to the back of the camper and got my bolt cutters and ran through the woods until I reached the building with the fence. I cut off the locks on the gate and building door. Inside the shed, were a lot tools...shovels, rakes and a bush axe. I grabbed the axe and headed back to the camper. By the time I got back, I was soaked in sweat and the meth was running through my veins at a thousand miles per hour. Kee was sitting in a yard chair in front of Carl cussing him as he gasped for air. Ralph was standing over Junior who was bleeding from the stab wound.

"I knocked Kee and the chair over. 'Enough of this shit. Let's get it over with.' I took a big swing with the bush axe and hit Carl right in the bridge of his nose. I was aiming at his neck but I missed. His eyes came out their sockets and brain matter shot all over my face and chest. The top half of his head hit the tree and because some of his skin was still attached, it just laid against the tree. His tongue and lower part of his face and chin were exposed.

"Kee got up off the ground and started throwing up. Rachel ran back to the camper screaming, 'Oh, my God! Oh, my God!' Ralph, knowing what was to come, walked away, and picked up the bottle of Jack.

"I walked over to Junior and took his head off with one swing.

I kicked the head toward the river. I was covered with blood, brain matter and sweat as I headed toward the water. With the bush axe in my hand, I walked into the river, and yelled, 'Yes, Baby, you don't have to worry about those sons-of-bitches anymore. Never again, Baby, never again. I love it, I simply love it!'

"My chest was pounding and now the spiders were gone. I washed off in the river and threw the bush axe downriver. I watched the axe sink as I headed back to the camper.

"When I woke up, I could feel the bouncing camper moving down the dirt road. I looked out the window and it was dark. I had been out for about five hours. Ralph had scouted around and found an old sewer line right-of-way. He said he had wrapped the bodies and parts in large garbage bags he had found in the shed. He had used a crowbar he'd found in the shed to remove the giant cast iron inspection covers which were located about three hundreds yard apart.

"He dumped the bodies into the holes and replaced the lids. Ralph did all of that while I was passed out on the floor of the camper. We returned to the campground where I took a shower and changed clothes. Both girls passed out and Ralph went outside to smoke a cigar.

"I knew what Ralph was going to say before he opened his mouth but I waited until he said, 'BH, what are we going to do about the girls? You know, even though they both participated, they are a risk and there is only one sure way to assure we have no witnesses.' I knew how he felt about Rachel so I tried to use it as leverage to save Kee. I said, 'What about Rachel? She is the first women you have ever shown any kind of compassion toward?'

"He took a big puff off his cigar and blew the smoke in my face. 'BH, do you want to sit in some electric chair or have some punk in a white smock stick a needle in your arm while twelve hypocritical bastards watch you choke on your own vomit. I don't think so, my friend.'

"I knew he was right. It would have to be done and done quickly."

After listening to the story of the slaughter near the river, it was time for a cigar. Once again I reflected upon my life as a lawman. One of the contributing factors involved in losing my career was the breaking of one of my own rules: Never trust anyone with a badge. I was a hands-on sheriff who stayed on top of everything and everyone who worked under me. I had more than 170 employees; most of them had worked for the former sheriff.

Soon after I was elected, I spoke with an old sheriff from eastern North Carolina. He had served for twenty-eight years. He had a small department with only twelve deputies. I had fired twenty-five deputies the first day I was in office and was criticized by the news media.

"How many did you fire, Sheriff?' I asked. He lit a cigar, tilted his straw hat, and said, 'I think it was five.'

"Any regrets?" I asked. He replied, 'Yes. I should have fired all of them.'

While I was sheriff, I spent a lot of time trying to convince politicians how bad the criminal world around us had become. So many of them didn't realize how bad things had become in recent years. They figured that the worst crime was somewhere else, not where they lived.

No longer was crime as simple as people trying to steal things or sell their bodies for profit. No longer was it the routine break-in cases where homes and businesses were looted.

Now the people committing these crimes were armed. These crooks were carrying guns with the intention of hurting someone. And the crooks were starting at a younger age. Fifteen-year-olds watching video games about bad guys shooting cops and driving off in their fast sports cars were getting bad ideas planted in their minds. Based on information I gathered from interviews, I learned that the young people of today's generation have no idea what the definition is for the word "no." And they see death as a character in a video game being torn to shreds with a machine gun. They see death as just that -- an animated drawing on the TV screen.

I walked around the lake and looked at the beautiful fields surrounding the old plantation. I imagined BH and Ralph being field bosses overlooking a hundred slaves. BH would be barking out orders and Ralph would be handing out punishment. Meanwhile, Cherokee would be sitting on the big front porch yelling, "Now Ralph, I think you need to go back over there and beat that one slave a little more."

Society has created hundreds of thousands of people like Ralph and BH. We think locking them up will solve the problem. We either don't put them in prison long enough or we put them away for too many years for minor offenses. They get educated by some of the most brilliant minds in America. These are "teachers" who were raised by brutal and abusive parents or relatives. Most were trapped in a world of hate and drug use. How in the hell do we expect them to be the same individuals as those of us who are the lucky ones?

I felt that I was growing soft in my old age, and I was again beginning to understand these sick bastards I had been hearing about for the last two days. Years ago, I would already have pulled out my pistol and shot them.

I made my way back over to Ralph and BH and took a swallow of sweet tea

"What happened next?" I asked BH, who was happy to continue.

He pulled a silver comb from his shirt pocket and began stroking his silver hair. "You know, Sheriff, after the killings at the river, I actually thought about getting out of the crime business and going straight. I wondered if I could live a normal life.

I put down my glass. "Why didn't you?" I asked.

BH slipped the comb back into his pocket. "I knew I was going to hell for what I already had done and the man upstairs wasn't going to let me slide just because I suddenly stopped, so why should I stop? Besides I liked killing. The hunt and the catch were my life.

"After we did away with the bodies, we headed north to Pennsylvania. I knew Ralph was going to pressure me about killing the girls but I had, in a weird way, grown fond of both girls. When we stopped at a truck stop just across the Pennsylvania state line, I asked Ralph to go inside and get some smokes while I filled up the van. I told the girls to get out and come with me.

"I spotted a young truck driver at the far end of the parking lot checking the load on his truck. Walking toward the trucker, I told the girls: 'Look, don't ask any questions and just go along with what I say.' They looked confused but knew better than to question anything I told them.

"The driver looked to be in his thirties and when he saw us approaching, he turned his attention to us. I reached out and shook his hand. 'Where are you heading, young fellow?' He said he was headed to Mississippi with a load of steel for the docks.

"He was a good looking fellow with long blonde hair and a muscular build. I could tell he was looking at the big breasts being exposed by Rachel. I told him the girls needed a ride to Mississippi and I would pay him to give the girls a ride. It was simply pure luck that he was heading to Mississippi because I knew Rachel had contacts there.

"Kee spoke up. 'What about our clothes?' I called them off to the side and said, "Look, Ralph doesn't trust you girls and you know what that means. I will get up with you later. Get your asses in the truck and go.' The young man was more than happy to take them off my hands.

"I gave the girls three-thousand dollars and the young trucker five-hundred dollars. I put my hand on the trucker's shoulder and told him the girls would look after him and to do whatever he wanted. They loaded up and in a few minutes disappeared down the highway.

By the time Ralph came out of the store, I had filled the tank. I quickly told him I had spotted a patrol car pulling into the parking lot. As soon as we got a couple of miles down the road, Ralph walked back to the bedroom. 'Where are the girls, BH?' he yelled. I pulled over on the side of the road and stood up. I knew better than to leave my back to him. I told him I had let the girls catch a southbound truck.

"He was a lot calmer than I expected and asked me if I knew where they were going. I told him somewhere in Mississippi. To my surprise, he was fine with it. We kept moving.

"Ralph had a friend who provided a place to park the camper. It was an old tobacco barn located on the backside of a farm owned by his friend's brother. They had converted the barn into a clubhouse for the local deer hunters. It had electricity and water with a small bath.

"His friend was big into guns and told us about a plan to steal several Civil War pistols from a museum near a battlefield. This sounded bizarre to me but according to Ralph's friend, these weapons were worth a lot of money. A foreign gun collector had offered nearly a million dollars if he could get the pistols he wanted.

"Ralph's friend had a sister who had worked at the museum several years ago. She told her brother that the locks on the gun cabinets weren't really locks at all. They were made to look like locks but were there for the convenience of the caretakers. The guns had to be cleaned and oiled every week, so the caretakers removed the real locks and replaced them with fake ones. This would make it possible for someone to reach over and get the guns out while another person distracted the guards.

"The brother and sister had been planning the theft for several years. The guy said, 'I just didn't have the guts to see it through.' Ralph and I were offered one-hundred-thousand dollars to carry out the robbery.

"It sounded like a good idea until we were told the heist would have to be carried out in broad daylight. Guards would be all over the place.

"We waited for three weeks while the woman gathered information from a museum guard she was dating. The guard wasn't in on the plot and suspected nothing. As most men do, he told the woman everything we needed to know about the guards' routine at the museum.

"Finally, on a cold, rainy day, we decided it was a good time to carry out our plan to rob the museum. Ralph and I would enter the museum wearing raincoats and toboggans. The woman helping us pull off the robbery had sewn large pockets on the insides of the raincoats. This gave us a place to put the guns when we pulled them out of the cabinets.

"Ralph's friend provided pictures of the cap and ball type pistols we were going after. There were a total of six pistols, all with very long barrels. I was really nervous about the whole thing. Ralph and I never liked to involve a lot of people in our work. The more people involved, the more chances you had of someone's talking.

"Before we left the farm, we looked at pictures of the museum, inside and out. The woman also had a diagram of all the cabinets and their locations.

"The woman, her brother, and Ralph and I headed to the museum in an old yellow Ford station wagon. It was the kind that had the sides covered with fake wood grain. White wall tires and wire hubcaps made it the perfect family looking vehicle.

"Not much was said on the drive over to the museum as we watched heavy fog sweep by the car. It made me think of all the men who probably had died on a day just like this during the Civil War. I felt like a Confederate spy on a secret mission to infiltrate a Union camp and kill its commander. I was always thinking strange stuff like that.

"By the time we arrived at the parking lot, the rain had turned into snow. I could see many of the visitors coming out of the battlefield seeking shelter. This is exactly what we wanted. Ralph looked over and gave me a wink. We got out of the station wagon and split up. I headed for a picnic shelter located across the street from the museum. Ralph went to the public restroom about fifty yards to the north. The brother went into the museum while the sister remained in the wagon.

"More people headed for the museum as the snow began to accumulate. I lit a smoke and waited about twenty minutes before crossing the street to enter the building. As I stepped off the curb, a delivery van came by and splashed water and snow on my pants leg. I gave him the driver a finger, not for the wet pants but because it made it easy for the guards to remember a guy with wet pants legs being in the building. I always tried to think of everything regardless of the type of crime.

"When I entered the building, I saw Ralph walking toward the back of the room which was packed with visitors. Men, women, and a few small kids were bunched together looking at the rifles on the walls. An old cannon sitting in the middle of the room was the centerpiece of the floor. The pistol cabinets were behind the cannon. Many of the visitors wearing heavy coats and holding umbrellas pushed their way around the room.

"According to the sister, two of the four guards took a break at 10 a.m. sharp. Glancing around the room, I located a big clock over the entrance door. It showed 9: 50. This would give us ten minutes to get the pistols or we would have to wait until eleven o'clock. Hanging around for an hour might draw suspicion from the guards.

"Ralph and I maneuvered over near the pistol cabinets and waited for the brother to cause a distraction. That was our way of getting the crowd's attention away from the pistol cabinet. While Ralph kept an eye on the crowd, I made a test pull on the cabinet doors and sure enough, they opened. I pushed them back shut and waited on the brother.

"He came in the front door with a large cup of coffee and in a matter of seconds, he spilled the coffee. 'Damn, I'm sorry!' he said aloud. One of the guards headed toward the back of the room to get a mop, and the other guard helped an elderly lady move out of the way of the spilled coffee.

"Ralph and I made our move. We snatched the pistols and quickly put them into the big pockets. We moved the remaining pistols closer together. Hopefully, this would give us some time before the guards noticed anything missing.

"The plan went smoothly. Ralph left first while I waited about ten minutes and met him at the station wagon. The brother joined us and we drove back to the farm where we had a discussion about what we would do with the pistols.

"According to the brother, it would take about a week to work the deal out with the money man. This being said, Ralph and I took three of the pistols with us as insurance. We didn't trust anyone when it came to money, especially a hundred grand.

"Before we left the farm, the brother and sister gave us ten-thousand dollars as good faith money. We didn't feel safe hanging around the farm. The brother gave us a phone number so we could call back and check on the status of the deal. We made it plain that we wanted to see the cash before we handed over the pistols.

"We headed for Pittsburgh where we parked the camper in a small campground just off the interstate. We waited for two weeks before contacting the brother and sister. I was told to meet a man at a local watering hole in Pittsburgh called Lories. This was a dive bar on the east side of town that I was familiar with. The place has been around since the thirties and has been handed down from family member to family member. Back in the heyday of the steel mills, it was a favorite hangout for workers after a hot day at the steel mill.

"Now it was a hangout for crack heads, whores and old bikers. I took a seat in the rear of the room with my back to the wall and waited. I was told the person I was to meet would be a white male in his fifties with a Scottish accent. I had a few drinks and around nine o'clock, this guy appeared. I sat there and waited to see if he approached me. He had been told I would be wearing a red baseball cap with a blue fish on it.

"He walked over to the table and took a seat. Supposedly, he hadn't been told my name and I was waiting to see if he knew my name. If he did, I'd know it was a setup.

"He had a heavy accent and I asked him several times to repeat what he said. We talked for about thirty minutes. I didn't have a good feeling about this guy. He was too refined in the way he asked questions concerning the weapons. This guy wasn't a criminal.

"He was trying to use language like a thug uses. You know, like I use. He was a cop and I could feel it to the bone. A damn sure way to find out if a guy is a cop is to keep playing him along until he gets pushy. That means he is wearing a wire and needs you to give him something he can use. He also has to be careful not to be accused of entrapment.

"This guy may have thought he was a good undercover man but I wasn't a rookie myself. I knew I had been in the crime business a lot longer than he had been in the cop business. I played dumb for most of the conversation and much to the cop's disgust, I left.

"Ralph had dropped me off nearly a mile away from the bar. I knew the man would have people waiting on me. I stepped outside, lit a cigarette, and looked around. It took a few minutes but I spotted one man standing on the corner and another one up the street beside a dark Ford sedan. Both looked like cops.

"Yes, I was going to be followed but I was banking on something I've always believed about cops. They are lazy, and they wouldn't follow me on foot. The snow and cold would keep them in their vehicles because they are creatures of habit. I left and walked down the street going in and out of bars until I finally slipped out the back door of one bar and lost them.

"As always, Ralph and I had a predetermined location to meet by a certain time. If I didn't show, he would go to the second spot and wait for thirty minutes. If I were still a no show, he would haul ass out of town. I met him at the first place and we headed out of town.

"Now we had a problem. We had three Civil War pistols and no one to buy them. We never had dealt with anything worth this kind of money. Drugs are one thing but an old pistol was just that to us, an old pistol. We waited a few days and contacted the brother and sister. They tried to play cool and act like they didn't know anything about the contact person being a cop. They insisted on a meeting so we could work out a deal on the pistols. But Ralph and I were too smart for that.

"We had our own plan. We stole a pickup truck and in the middle of the night, drove to a location near the farm. We walked for about a mile and went down to the house where the brother and sister lived. A small light was on in the kitchen. Ralph stayed at the front door while I made my way around to the back porch. The sister's bedroom was off to the left of the sliding glass doors. I had seen her hide the key under a flower pot when we were in the back yard smoking dope.

"I slid the door open and stepped inside. From the hallway, I could see the light from the television in her room flickering under the door. As I approached the door, I pulled my pistol from my belt and held it close to my ear. I eased the wood paneled door slowly inward and stepped inside. On the four poster bed, I could see two bodies. One was the sister and the other was the man from the bar... the undercover cop. The man was completely nude and the girl was partially under him with one arm on his shoulder and the other underneath the pillow.

"I stood there and thought of how the little bitch had double-crossed us and now was planning to rip us off. My first thought was to blow them away but I knew that might cause other problems. Her connections with the boyfriend and also with the museum could hinder our efforts to sell the pistols. I backed out the door and found Ralph. We agreed it would be best to keep the hot pistols and move on.

Chapter Fifteen

Hot Pistols Find New Home

"Ralph and I left the area and headed toward New York. We knew we could find a fence to get rid of the antique pistols. We might not get the money we had hoped for but New York is a place where anything can be bought or sold.

"We stopped off in the little town of Canastota, New York, the home of the National Boxing Hall of Fame. Ralph had been a boxer in prison and had known a fellow inmate who was a boxer and now owned a small gym in this little town. He contacted his friend Colt, a former Golden Gloves boxer, and arranged to meet him.

"Colt had gone straight for several years after he was released from prison, but he'd had a relapse to his drug addiction. The gym was located in an old high school building he'd bought from the county years before. Colt trained several young boys who wanted to be selected for the Golden Gloves tournaments.

"We only wanted to stay there for a few nights but we stayed for about three weeks. The town was made up of a lot of old retired people, and many of the residents worked for the state. They paved and maintained the highways in the spring and summer and spent winters down at the local union hall drinking and smoking.

"Ralph and I spent a lot of time shooting pool at the local pubs, but there were no scores for the few young girls we saw. Colt wanted us to rob the owner of a nearby resort but we nixed that idea. Ralph hadn't seen Colt for several years and didn't feel good about his ideas. We left the place in the middle of the night without telling Colt we were leaving.

"Once in New York City, we parked the camper behind the old body shop where I used to work. We made some contacts and quickly found out the guns would be hard to move. We needed to make contacts with some of the rich types in the heart of the city. After a week, Ralph found a fence that had a man who wanted to see the guns. He was an old Jewish man who ran a pawnshop. It was an upscale place that dealt mostly in jewelry, gold, and silver.

"We were told to go to the back of the store and wait to be buzzed in. We took one pistol and hid it behind the dumpster in the alley behind the store in case the cops were waiting on us in the shop. In a few minutes, the buzzer sounded and we entered the old red brick building. Standing in the hall was an old man dressed in a wrinkled black suit, a white shirt, and a bright red tie. His black horned rim glasses pushed up against thick grey eyebrows. He seemed to have a habit of rubbing his large nose. The man was bent over and used a black cane to help him walk into a small cluttered office.

"The room was dark with a small floor lamp in the corner. He took a seat behind the mahogany desk and pulled out a picture of one of the pistols we had taken. "Is this the weapon you have? He turned the picture around for us to see. Both of us nodded in his direction and remained standing. He raised both arms and motioned for us to take a seat. 'You know, gentleman, if you indeed possess this weapon, you have a very valuable piece of history. People are going to be very upset about losing such a piece. With all that being said, I would like to see this weapon.'

"Ralph told him to go out into the alley and we would show him the weapon. In case this may be a trap, we didn't want to handle the weapon or give it to him. Once we reached the alley, Ralph pushed the small dumpster away from the wall and pointed to the black bag on the ground.

"The old man reached down and slowly pulled the pistol out of the bag. We could hear him saying, 'Nice, very nice. Indeed.' He took the pistol, slid it into the bag, and placed it back on the ground. He looked up and said, 'I will be touch with you in two hours and make you an offer, a onetime offer only.'

"We left the old man and went down to a bar and waited. He had given us a number to call when the time was up. It started to rain as we walked down the street and by the time we reached the bar, it was pouring. Ralph and I talked about how creepy the old man had been. Both of us were looking for signs of being followed. We split up and looked for cops.

"There was a bar across the street from the old man's place. I took a seat at the window of the bar and watched in both directions for anything or anyone looking suspicious. In a strange way, we had to act like detectives looking for a bad guy in order to counter any cops who might be involved with a surveillance squad. We knew they would have to see us hand the guns over to secure a conviction.

"The two hours passed and I went to a phone booth and made the call. The old man answered on the third ring. He told me he had one-hundred-thousand dollars cash and to call him back in twenty minutes with our answer. I had the answer but he wouldn't talk to me and just told me to call back in twenty minutes. Ralph had stepped outside under an awning to smoke. I moved closer to the window and gave him thumbs up and he returned it with one of his own.

"When I called the old man, he instructed me to take a cab to an address down in the Bronx and look for a black Mercedes sedan parked on the corner. It was a short ride down to the corner and the Mercedes was just where it was supposed to be.

"We exited the cab and spotted the old man sitting on a small bench near what appeared to be the yard of a church. Ralph stayed at the corner and I walked across the street. The old man had a newspaper in his hands and told me to have a seat. He placed his hand on my leg and told me to walk over to a swing set nearby. The money would be in a briefcase inside the trash can next to the swing. Once I verified the money was inside, I was to give him a nod and signal to Ralph to bring the pistols across the street and place them on the bench. The deal went down and Ralph and I were on our way.

"We drove out of town and didn't stop until we were able to find a rest stop. We took the money from the case and looked for any tracking device which possibly could be in the money. The money was used and we found nothing. We threw the briefcase into a trash can near the parking lot.

"As always, we split the money right there and headed down the interstate. It wasn't long until Ralph started asking about the girls. I knew he wouldn't rest until he found them. I also knew he would probably kill them both and maybe me, as well. I started putting a plan through my mind to split from Ralph for a while. Stealing guns from a federally operated museum was going to bring a lot of heat.

"After a little talking, I convinced Ralph it would be a good idea to take me back to the body shop. I would stay there and work for a while. He agreed and dropped me off at the shop, then headed south to look for the girls. I had no way of warning them so they were on their own.

"I bought an old Ford from my friend at the body shop. It used to be a police cruiser and had been painted black. My friend had used it to move dope and money through the city. The thinking was that people, including the cops, would think it was a detective vehicle.

"I decided to head down near the North Carolina coast and looked up my old friend Lonny who had a large track of land that was used by tree farmers to grow pines. In the old days he made moonshine back in the woods but now he was old and lived alone in a modest home. His place was near an area known as Green Swamp. About the only visitors he had were deer and bear hunters.

"Lonny and I became friends in federal prison in Atlanta where he was pulling two years. Again the prison family connections had made it possible for me to lay low. Lonny liked to fish and had a real nice boat that was more like a ship than a boat. This thing was a huge thirty-footer. The first time we went out on that boat, Lonny said, 'Not bad for a poor old country boy. The second time we went out, he had his nephew with him. He was a big old red neck kid named Dowdy, and he appeared to have some mental issues. He never wore a shirt with his bibbed overalls and his bare feet.

"One night when we had passed the breakers, Lonny told me we were going to meet another boat and unload some cargo. When the boat arrived, Dowdy tied up with it while Lonny talked to a couple of Mexicans. It wasn't long until we were taking a load of pot on board. Over a hundred and fifty kilos were loaded onto Lonny's boat. Lonny and one of the Mexicans went below for a few minutes and the Mexican soon left with a large pillowcase.

"I laughed and thought how Lonny, who had to be at least 80, was still in the business. 'Once you have had the taste of a hundred, it's hard to go back to a twenty,' I thought.

"There were a couple vans waiting at Lonny's house, and we loaded the pot onto the vans. There I was right in the middle of the drug business. I knew I couldn't stay and get caught in the middle of it. Just like any other business, I knew it would be only a matter of time before all parties involved would get greedy and eventually would be robbing and killing each other.

"Old Lonny was moving a ton of pot per month and his network was large. It covered at least twenty-five counties in North Carolina and a few in South Carolina.

Chapter Sixteen

No Witnesses Left Behind

"Lonny asked me to serve as his cash collector for five grand a week. I agreed only because he had been good to me. His customers had been with him for many years and picking up the money usually was just a matter of making a few calls. The money would be picked up at a predetermined location. I never had to meet anyone. They dropped the money off at different locations...parks, rest stops and telephone poles in the middle of nowhere. They never saw me and I never saw them. The old man had a good system and it was easy on me.

"Though easy, it also was boring. My appetite for action, including sex, started calling me to service. I couldn't stand to be safe; I needed danger and missed my old pal Ralph and the girls. I told the old man I would have to go and he thanked me for my work. He gave me ten grand for a job well done. He had one last collection for me. A man down in South Carolina was behind in his payments and owed him a hundred-thousand dollars. Lonny hadn't heard from him in more than two months.

"Lonny instructed me to find him and collect the money or see that he never owed anyone else again. Before I left, he gave me a pillowcase and told me it was for expenses. Once in the car, I looked into the pillowcase and found another ten thousand dollars, a .357 Magnum pistol, and a box of shells. On a sheet torn from a yellow legal pad was information about the man along with a picture of him.

"I left and made the short trip across the state line. I quickly found the address of the client. His very nice house was way back off the road across the street from a small strip mall which gave me a perfect place to case the house. I had no sooner parked when I saw a red Mercedes pull into the driveway and stop. A short stocky man with a large beer belly got out of the car and walked to the mailbox. His full head of gray hair caused him to look to be in his fifties.

"The information sheet noted that he lived with his trophy girlfriend and didn't have kids. As I watched him drive up to the house, I decided I would come back around midnight and do the deal. I sure did miss old Ralph and the girls at a time like this. I watched him pull into the garage and lower the door. He came out of a side door and headed toward the house. I took the pistol and put it in the arch of my back and headed up to the house.

I knew I wouldn't leave him alive regardless whether he paid the money or not. I also knew what I would do with the girlfriend if she were there. All of these tough guys were the same. Leave him alive and he will have you tracked down just like he was tracked down.

"I pulled my car to a parking space near the fence at the swimming pool. I could see him sitting at a table with a dark haired woman in a bright orange bikini. Both had a drink in their hand.

"As I got out of the car, the man got up and headed toward the fence. He wanted to know if he could help me with anything. I told him I was looking for a body repair place and had been told it was close to the strip mall. He hesitated a moment and informed me he wasn't aware of any. I thanked him and started back to the car. Before I opened my car door, he yelled, 'I have a friend who works on cars. I can get his number if you like.' I said, 'Sure' and we walked by the pool and into the house. The woman followed us inside and walked over to the kitchen sink.

"When he reached for a drawer beside the sink, I pulled my

pistol and put it to his head. The woman just stood there with the drink in her hand. I told him I was there to collect some money owed to the old man. I told him if he didn't have money he would die.

"'Ok, Ok, I understand. Calm down. I have the money,' he said. The woman asked him what the hell was going on and he quickly told her, 'Shut the hell up.' I told the woman to turn around and put her hands behind her. I handcuffed her and told her to get on her knees. She started crying and the man told her to calm down. I reached over to the sink and picked up a green washcloth and stuck it in her mouth. I told the man to turn around and I put the second set of cuffs on him.

"I used wire ties to tie the woman's ankles together. By this time, she was crying like crazy. The man led me down the hall and went to the bedroom. He pulled the mattress off and showed me a pillowcase filled with what appeared to be cash. He handed it to me and as soon as I looked inside, I could tell it should be enough to cover the debt. I pulled back the hammer and shot him right between the eyes. His brains flew out the back and covered the wall behind him. He fell on the floor, eyes wide open.

"When I returned to the kitchen, the woman was trying to crawl to the back door. I picked her up by her long ponytail and pulled her down the hall. Her top came down revealing two large brown breasts. This excited me and the adrenaline rush was now at its highest level. I took her into the bedroom and when she saw her lover on the floor, despite the rag in her mouth, she tried to scream. I could see the fear in her eyes.

"I pulled the mattress away from the bed. It had brain matter and blood on it so I flipped it over. I pulled her over onto the mattress and placed the barrel of the gun on her neck and said, 'I'm going to take the rag out of your mouth. Do you understand me?' She nodded to indicate she did. 'Do you want to live?' I said as I unbuckled my belt. She again nodded 'yes.' Standing there naked, I told her if she made a sound, I would blow her head off. Again, she nodded.

"I slowly pulled the rag out of her mouth and she took a deep breath, sucking in as much air as she could. I stuck the rag back into her mouth and told her to stay put. I walked over to a desk sitting near the window and found a legal pad and pen. While taking the handcuffs off her hands, I told her, 'Take this pad and pen and write down everything you want me to do to you.' She looked up and reached with her shaking hands to take them. I stood in front of her and placed my manhood on her face and said, 'Don't leave anything out.'

"I went back to kitchen and got a couple of beers from the refrigerator. When I returned to the bedroom, the woman was busy writing. Her hands were shaking and tears were running down to her breast. She had a great body...firm breasts, flat stomach and long legs. I knew I was going to enjoy myself.

"Her body was trembling. I reached over and pulled the blue bow out of her hair. I took a seat in a small black chair with a white cushion, popped the top off the beer and took a sip and watched her write down her wishes. In my mind, I knew she was really enjoying this. She had probably watched a thousand movies and pictured herself as being the victim. Now was her chance to have it all come true. I knew she wanted it.

"She was bent over with the paper on her thighs and her long hair hid her face. She had stopped crying and would push her hair back behind her ear. That turned me on. Her hair also partially exposed the side of her breast and I wanted to just go over and lick them but I refrained and drank the beer.

"As I watched her write, I tried to imagine what was going through her head. Did she actually think I would let her go? Maybe I would take her with me to live out a life of crime as I did the girls? I did think of taking her with me. But she didn't look like the type. She looked too sophisticated. She probably was educated.

"I took a sip of the beer and asked, 'Are you ready to?' She raised her head and looked at me with those big blue eyes. 'I guess so. I never have been asked to write things down,' she said. I reached over and took the paper from her hand. I sat back in the chair and read them out loud.

"I will perform oral sex on you first and then you can do me. Then we can do it to each other. Then you can do me from behind, if you like that. I also like to be spanked and talked to. I will do whatever you want. I promise.'

"I handed the paper back to her and told her to read them back to me, and she did. I walked over to her and pulled her hair back and looked down at her. She was inches from my shaft. I took the pistol and shot her in the top of her head and watched her fall to the mattress. I took another a sip of beer, gathered the cans, and left.

"I took the money back to the old man and headed toward Louisiana. I needed to find Ralph and see if we could get another boat and work around the gulf doing fishing charters. I now had a contact with the old man to move some pot to North Carolina.

"I finally was able to get in touch with Ralph, and we made arrangements to meet in Mississippi where I met him at a small motel just outside of Hattiesburg.

"He still had the old van so I took the Ford that I had been driving down to the river, opened the doors, and rolled it into the river to watch it sink. Now we had to find the girls. We drove down to the coast and checked out some old hangouts. We knew by now the girls would have established a hangout so we just had to find it."

Chapter Seventeen

Mississippi Spells Trouble

BH stretched his arms as he sat in the wheelchair. It was as if he were getting tired.

"I've got to finish this part before we take a break," he said and continued his story.

"We had driven only a few miles on Interstate 10 when a state trooper pulled us over. He checked Ralph's driver's license and walked back to his cruiser. He said he stopped us because we didn't have any tail lights. Ralph told me the trooper was lying because he had checked the lights before we'd left the motel.

"Suddenly, more trooper cars pulled up with lights flashing. One car stopped behind us and one to the side. They had us boxed in and both of us knew this wasn't a routine traffic stop. The troopers were armed with shotguns and told us to come outside with our hands up. We knew right then, we were in deep shit.

"It seems that the sister and brother in Pennsylvania had ratted us out about the gun heist. We were facing serious time. There wasn't any use to try and shoot our way out. We got out of the car with our hands high in the air.

"We were handcuffed and taken to a federal jail. Each of us took a plea bargain for five-year sentences. I ended up in a Kansas prison and Ralph landed in Atlanta. We considered ourselves lucky with those light sentences. Our ages were a factor in the judge's decision. We had been more worried about being charged with the killings, but nothing had been mentioned about them. That's the way the feds work. As long as they get a conviction that makes them look good, they're happy.

"As soon as I arrived at the prison, I started looking look for a way to escape. I had spent enough time behind bars to know that I wouldn't survive in there as an old man. Even if I were caught trying to escape, I would be moved to a smaller and more private cell and only catch six months extra on my sentence.

"It was in the winter of my second year when my chance to bust out finally came. I had a job in maintenance and had free movement of the prison. I even had seen the blueprints of the prison on several occasions while doing maintenance work. The duct system for the heating unit became my avenue to the outside.

"A big snowstorm hit the area for three days straight dumping nearly three feet of snow. I started a large fire in the laundry room by taking a dozen sheets and putting them into the dryer. I had soaked them with penetrating oil from the machine shop. Once the sheets got really hot, they burst into flames. Since I had removed the dryer exhaust system hoses and attached them to the heat ducts, smoke soon filled the duct system. The eruption of the smoke caused the guards to order all inmates in my section out into the yard and into the snow.

"My plan worked but the dryer caught on fire. That started a fire in the entire laundry room which set the sprinkler system off. While the guards were trying to remove the inmates, a riot broke out. All hell broke loose. The National Guard was called out and everything just went crazy.

"While in the yard, I spotted a big National Guard truck. I looked inside and saw that a guardsman had left a big coat on the seat. I put the coat on, and soon after a prison guard yelled at me to move the truck outside of the walls. I jumped in and drove it right out. I just kept on driving for about fifty miles before I spotted a truck pull over area.

"I left the truck and almost immediately was able to hop another ride on the back of a tractor-trailer rig that was pulling out of the truck parking area. I jumped onto the back and climbed under the canvas cover. It was one of those open kinds of truck beds. When the truck neared a truck stop outside of St. Louis, I jumped from the truck. Another trucker gave me a ride to Birmingham, Alabama and from there I made my way to New Orleans."

Tired of standing, I took a seat. "BH, do you consider yourself lucky in that none of the killings ever came up when you were arrested for other offenses," I asked.

"Well, sheriff, you know the old saying, if they don't ask, you don't tell." I nodded in agreement, knowing the code of the bad guys. Keep your mouth shut.

Ralph stood and told me the nurse was coming back out to the house to give BH another breathing treatment. He asked if I would like to go fishing with him down at the big lake on the backside of the plantation. The lake was almost fifty acres and had some good fishing, he said. I would be glad to get away from BH for a while so I quickly agreed. Ralph and I headed towards the lake.

When we arrived at the lake, I saw it was just what I expected. There was an old fishermen's hut built out of logs from southern pines. It had a slate roof covered with green moss and had two bedrooms, a kitchen, a living room, and a den with a large fireplace.

Ralph said he went down to the lake when BH was having treatments or at times when he wanted time alone. About fifty yards from the house was a small boathouse, and inside was a sixteen-foot wooden fishing boat. It was old and powered by a thirty five-horsepower Mercury motor.

"You fly fish, Sheriff?" he asked as he handed me a wooden fly rod. I told him I had been fly fishing several times but wasn't the greatest at it.

The lake was beautiful and naturally fed by three springs. Ralph took the boat up to the watershed. This is where slaves used to load water onto wagons and take it out in the fields to water the cotton plants, he said. He reached into the small cooler he had brought along and handed me a cold beer. We fished for a while and caught some really nice largemouth bass and some giant yellow perch.

Ralph pulled the boat along the bank and we got out near a small picnic shelter. He placed the cooler on a handmade table and offered me another beer. I was getting a little nervous about being out in the middle of nowhere with a stone-cold killer. I had my Ka-bar knife and was prepared for anything, and I made a point to always keep Ralph in front of me.

Ralph lit a cigar, offered me one, and started talking. "You know, Sheriff, I was wondering what you are going to do with all this information BH and I have given you? You could go to the cops or write one hell of a book."

I lit my cigar and told him he was right about both ideas but I didn't have intentions of going to the police. I gave my word. Beside I had been out of the business for a long time and really didn't owe anything to anyone.

Writing a book was a possibility but I probably would wait until he and BH were dead, I said. I told him I had no idea how long I was going to be around myself. Ralph took a big puff of his cigar, and said, "Yep. That makes sense."

"Ralph, do you mind if I ask you a few questions?" I said. "I find you to be a very unique individual and would like to learn some things from you." He tapped the ashes off his cigar and told me to go ahead and ask away.

"What happened after BH escaped from prison? I assume you two guys got back together." Ralph lifted one foot off the ground and placed it on the table. He said, "BH got down to New Orleans and after about a week, a friend of mine told me he had seen BH in a pool hall off Bourbon Street. I knew the place, and I drove down several times and parked across the street for a couple of hours. Finally, I saw BH walk into the building. I found him shooting a game of nine balls by himself.

"We left and went to a rundown apartment on the south side and discussed what we needed to do. I had been released from prison early and had heard about BH escaping from Kansas. I knew he would head to New Orleans to find the girls."

"What about the girls?" I asked.

"Of course, BH wanted to know if I had found them, which I hadn't. I had gone to Hattiesburg but they had already left. They were supposed to be in New Orleans. I was working on a shrimp boat and didn't have time to look for them," he said.

"Sheriff, do you really want to hear something crazy?"

"What's that, Ralph?"

"You remember the van? You know the cops seized it the night they took us down," Ralph said. It seems my lawyer got it released back to me while I was gone. I had it parked down near the docks. Crazy shit, huh?"

As I watched some ducks slowly land on the lake, I said, "Well, tell me more about the girls. Did you find them?

Ralph had pulled out his knife and started cleaning the bass we caught.

"Oh yes. You know we found them. They were working in the casino down by the river. They were walking the floor and carrying drinks. They were shocked to see me walk in."

I thought, "I bet they were."

Ralph said, "BH was laying low down near the docks. He contacted some guy up in North Carolina about helping him get a boat so he could haul pot. They worked out a deal, and the boat was delivered by a couple of Mexicans. It took us a few weeks to clean it up and then we started moving pot for the old man."

Chapter Eighteen

On the Road Again

"We took the girls down to the docks and talked things over," Ralph said. "BH was worried about me harming the girls but I assured them I was over that. I had pulled my time and knew they would be putting themselves behind bars if they ran their mouths."

Listening to Ralph was a bit different than listening to BH whose voice had held a tone of finality. BH was relating what he called his confession. Ralph's stories were only filling in some gaps so that I understood the "big story" of how he and BH had gone through hell together while Ralph was anxious to tell about the reunion.

"Within a couple of months, the girls were making the runs with us on the boat and it was just like old times. We figured as long as we spent most of our time on the boat, BH would be okay. We also knew the feds would give up hunting him after a while. They just don't have the resources to keep on looking for people. We got BH a new ID and he let his hair grow real long and grew a beard. It didn't take each of us long to get back on the shit either. The girls were still on crack so we spent a lot of our money on dope just like before.

"We got back on our feet by running pot and then bought a bigger boat. We also did some charter fishing in order to get familiar with the Coast Guard. They stopped us a few times on the charters but usually were more interested in the girls than the boat or us."

I interrupted Ralph to ask about something that had been on my mind since BH had begun his confession: "I figure you guys were involved in more violent crimes than you have told me about."

Ralph replied, "That isn't exactly true, Sheriff. We did well for almost a year until we met with the old man in North Carolina. He offered us one million dollars to take a load of cocaine down to a little island off the coast of Belize. It was a place called Coker Cay. It turned out to be one hell of a job. We almost got our ass hung out in the middle of the jungle."

I was really interested in that story. "Tell me what happened," "I said.

Ralph was busy placing the cleaned fish into the cooler and then had to open another beer before he resumed the story.

"Lonny, the old man, gave us fifty thousand dollars up front and a map showing the location of the island. Tourists frequented the island which mainly had small shops and restaurants. You could rent golf carts and four-wheelers but there were only a few cars and no paved streets or roads.

"We arrived there around midnight and were met by some native islanders. I couldn't tell if they were Mexicans or blacks. They spoke Spanish and English. We took our boat and followed them around to the back of the island where a few more men were waiting on us at a small pier situated below a cliff. There were steps leading up the hill to a house at the top. Rachel and Kee followed behind us. Both had their pistols in their purses. BH and I also had our pistols in our belts in plain sight.

"The house wasn't a shack by any means. It was made of bamboo and had a thatched roof. A man speaking French...I think that's what it was...met us. He quickly switched to English but he wasn't very good at it. Still, you could tell he was *the* man. He invited us in and had a meal prepared which was served by a couple of good-looking native girls. The girls weren't wearing tops and were showing real nice tits.

"After dinner, the Frenchman put some coke on the bar. Kee and Rachel dived into the coke and within a few minutes were loose as a goose. The girls pulled their tops off and started messing around with the other two girls. They put on some Rolling Stones' music and started dancing around near the pool.

"The Frenchman asked about the money. BH told him we had it but we wanted to see the rest of the coke. The Frenchman looked over at one his men and signaled him to bring it in. They returned shortly with a hand truck with about ten kilos on it.

"BH pulled out his knife and quickly cut into the coke and snorted a line. He then handed me some coke on the tip of the knife and I snorted it right up. It was some good stuff.

"BH told me to go down to the boat and bring up the money. When I returned, the Frenchman and all of the girls were naked in the pool. I knew BH would not take part and I didn't want to get in. I was ready to get the hell out of there. The Frenchman kept feeding the girls coke and before long, things started to get out of hand.

"I knew BH didn't like what was happening and things could get bad at the drop of a hat. The native guys mixed some rum drinks for BH and me. Rachel and Kee finally got out of the pool knowing all well that BH wouldn't take that shit very long.

"Kee could speak Spanish and overheard the Frenchman telling one of his men to wait down at the boat and shoot us when got down there. BH and I walked to the far end of the pool and figured a way to get them before they got us.

"The Frenchman got out of the pool, put on a white silk robe, and headed over to the bar. I followed him and asked his man to pour me a tall rum. BH went over to the door with Kee and Rachel and told them to get dressed. The girls picked up their purses knowing exactly what was about to go down. As soon as I saw them open their purses, I pulled my pistol and shot the Frenchman in the back of the head. One of his men pulled a pistol and Kee shot him three times in the stomach. Another guy burst through the door and Rachel shot him in the chest. He fell hard to the floor.

"The two girls in the pool started screaming and BH went over and shot each of them about five times. The pool turned red as we gathered up the dope and the money. When we tried to leave the house, someone on the outside opened up with an automatic rifle.

"I went out by the pool and made my way around the house. I watched until I saw the muzzle flash. While the man was shooting at the house, I made a run toward him. He never saw me coming and I tackled him. He dropped the rifle as we rolled down the hill. As we stopped rolling, I started stabbing him until he passed out. I found his rifle and went back and shot him in the mouth.

"I could see BH and the girls heading down the steps toward the boat. I met them there. We untied the boat, fired it up, and headed out. About a half of a mile out, we spotted a light headed toward us at high speed. We knew it was some of the guys from the estate. BH and Rachel went down below and brought up three AR-15s. Kee took over the wheel while Rachel, BH, and I waited for the smaller boat to approach us. We knew we couldn't outrun them so we prepared to fight for our lives.

"As soon as the boat got closer, they started firing at us. We headed toward the shore about a mile away. Although we couldn't out run them, we thought if we could put the shore to our back they might hesitate to shoot since there were houses on the shoreline. As soon as they got near us, the three of us opened up with the rifles and knocked out their light. We saw one crew member fall overboard.

"As they were making a turn, BH put about twenty rounds into the gas tank area and the engine burst into flames. I took over the wheel and headed our boat toward them. They were jumping off the burning boat. We pulled closer and it was like shooting fish in a barrel. There were five of them. We killed all of them and left them for the sharks.

"Kee had taken a bullet to the arm and was bleeding pretty bad so we headed toward the island of San Pedro. We pulled into the marina, tied off, and went looking for a doctor. Rachel stayed with the boat.

"BH and I found a couple guys at the end of the dock and gave them a hundred-dollars apiece to give us some information and put us in a golf cart. We headed toward the slum section of town. An old lady came to the door of one of the huts and told us to come in. It was one of those places where there are chickens on the couch and pigs in the bedroom. To say it was nasty would have been an understatement.

"The old women knew what she was doing and dug the bullet out of Kee in no time. We gave her three-hundred-dollars and headed back to the docks. When we returned, Rachel was talking to a man near the boat. It seems we had taken a round in the fuel tank. The man said he could fix it in the morning when he could get some parts.

"We hung around on the boat until daylight and the man showed up with a couple of kids. He wanted a one-hundred dollars to go back into town and buy the parts. San Pedro is in a Third World Country. The place looked like a haven for thugs and killers... people like us. Everyone looked at you as though they wanted to kill you or eat you.

"I decided to go into town with the local guys who were going after the parts. We had to stop at a toll bridge in order to get into to town. A policeman helping the toll bridge attendant walked over to the golf cart and asked the men what they were up to. They knew him but he gave me a look and wanted to know where I came from. I told him I had trouble with my boat and needed some parts. The guys knew him and we were on our way without a problem. I was nervous about these guy, but I had to have the parts!

"We bought the parts and as we returned near the bridge, the guys in the cart with me said I would have to tip the guard if I wanted to get back without more questions. I gave him a twenty and we were allowed to pass. The repairs took about two hours and we were on our way,

"We had a million dollars in cash and five to ten million dollars' worth of coke. We also knew by now the old man had been contacted about the deal. We would need to be careful about how we approached him. Thugs think alike so we needed to have a plan. Hopefully, he would only want the dope and wouldn't give a damn about the cash.

"We met the old man out at sea. He took the dope and told us he had indeed been contacted about the deal. He advised the people he would contact them if we showed up. We gave him the dope and headed back down the eastern seaboard toward New Orleans.

"After getting to New Orleans, we headed up the Mississippi River. Rachel knew of a house for rent right on the river. It belonged to another drug dealer. I was sure she had been doing him but at this point I didn't care. With a million dollars I could put up with anything.

"We arrived at the house around 10 p.m. and Rachel went to the door while we tied off the boat. Rachel came back with a guy wearing a white hat and white suit. He looked like one of those guys you see walking around the French Quarter. The house was nice with big columns and a front porch. It was run-down but was hidden among large magnolia trees.

"The guy wanted thirty-five hundred a month for the place but I got him down to three grand. We paid him for a year. The place was fully furnished with what looked to be 1980s furniture. It was two stories with a wraparound veranda. It could be made into a nice place but we knew we would never stay along enough to fix it up.

"The owner of the house came the next night and had a couple of hot chicks and some blow with him. All of us started drinking and snorting and before long we got into a discussion about swinging with the girls. The guy wanted to know if BH and I would be into watching the girls do each other. Normally, the answer would be no but we all were strung out and I knew it was going to happen.

"Rachel and Kee were all in and it was only a few minutes until all of us were upstairs in the big room. It had once been a dance room but had been converted into a large dining hall with several couches. There was a huge Confederate flag hanging on the wall above the fireplace. Between the flag and the fireplace was a large portrait of Andrew Jackson at the Battle of New Orleans. I thought the scene was a bit ironic since we had robbed a museum for Civil War pistols.

"We soon learned that our landlord was a city councilman in a small parish nearby. That worried me at first but I knew he was also a crime boss of sorts with a lot of connections. The party continued on through the night and by daylight, we had consumed all the dope and booze.

"The New Orleans Police Department had a long history of corruptness and with help from the landlord, we made several contacts with them. It wasn't long until the councilman and his girls became frequent visitors to the house. We went out on the boat and drank and did blow several times. I didn't like the attention but we soon established a little drug business with some of the rich and famous. Politicians, cops, bankers, you name it, we supplied them.

"All drug deals were done from the boat. We would meet on the river where their boat pulled alongside our boat. We delivered the goods and they gave us the money. BH and I knew it would be only a matter of time until a big drug kingpin would hear about someone moving in on his territory. After about six months it happened.

"We were on the river waiting for the councilman when two low-riding speedboats approached and came alongside. There was a driver and two other guys on the one boat that pulled close to us. There were two black men and a slim white man who appeared to be in his fifties. He was sharply dressed in blue slacks and white polo style shirt. His grey hair was slicked back above his round tanned face. He asked to come aboard and we agreed that only he could board the vessel. He agreed while his friends moved toward the front of their boat.

"He said his name was Louis Centell and he was a shipping broker in New Orleans. It didn't take him long to explain how it was rumored that we were conducting a business in his area. We talked for a while and came to the understanding that we would pay a small fee for use of what he called 'his river.' We gave him a down payment of two grand. BH and I knew this guy was going to be trouble. I told BH we should just turn around and kill them all.

"Our business started growing and before long, we were pulling down two hundred grand a week. The old man back in North Carolina loved it and even came down to visit. Once we told him of the fees which had now grown to over five grand a week, he wanted to meet this Louis guy.

"It was strange to see the old man with his bib overalls sitting on the back of the boat talking to the refined Mr. Centell. Both were smoking Cubans, and Mr. Centell was wearing his white summer suit and tie. Mr. Centell quickly found out that although the old man looked like a hillbilly farmer, he knew how to make a deal. They were quite the odd couple and within a few weeks, we were moving a ton of coke a month.

"By now the girls had fallen in love with the lifestyle and new friends. They never had been around society types, and they loved having new clothes and socializing.   "BH and I were growing tired of it all and decided we had to move on. We knew it wouldn't be easy to quit the business. These guys expect you to sign on for life or as they put it, 'once you're in the family, you're in it for until you die or just disappear.'

"We had enough money that even we should be able to live a good life for a very long time. We decided we would make one last score with Mr. Centell.

"We took the boat and headed down to New Orleans to meet Mr. Centell for our usual transfer of coke for cash. This was unusual because we always had met up river away from the city.

Chapter Nineteen

Out Foxing the Drug Boss

"We left the girls back at the house to prepare for a party they were having for a few of their girlfriends. On the way past the city we observed an ocean liner coming in escorted by tug boats. Two police vessels were behind the ocean liner. As we passed, one of the police boats peeled off and started following us.

"We were carrying ten kilos of coke and though hidden very well, we knew if they boarded, it could get nasty. After a half of mile they turned the blue lights on and headed our way. I went below to get an AR-15 but BH yelled and told me they were going past us. They went by us at a very high rate of speed and stopped a small fishing boat just off shore.

"Like always, BH had a feeling about things and we continued on to one of the docks. Mr. Centell's boat was tied off the dock and we pulled in behind it. He was waiting outside near a small foreman's shack at the top of the ladder. He had his two bodyguards with him. He and the bodyguards came aboard and he asked to see the dope. Usually, he would show the money and then demand to see the dope but this time he wanted to see the dope first. BH quickly told him there would not be a deal unless we saw the money first.

"One of his guards pulled out his pistol and told us, 'You heard the man. Get the dope.' They had the drop on us and I knew what

BH's response would be. 'No way. Show us the money or we leave,' he said as he stood up. Mr. Centell told his man to search the boat and I was thinking we were going to be shafted. They said they didn't have any money and were going to blow our heads off as soon as they found the dope.

"Mr. Centell pulled out his pistol, a chrome .45 caliber automatic, and told the other goon to help his partner look for the drugs. As soon as he disappeared down the steps, I made a lunge at Mr. Centell and both of us went overboard. As soon as we came to the surface I heard three shots ring out above. I punched Mr. Centell in the face several times and heard his nose break on the last punch. He dropped the pistol and the briefcase floated by my head as he began to choke. I got him in a headlock as he frantically gasped for air. He gave up and I told him to get up the ladder. On the way up, I heard two more shots go off.

"In a few seconds, BH came to the side of the boat and grabbed Mr. Centell's hand and pulled him up. I took the fish net and lifted the brief case out of the water and to my surprise, the money was inside. We knew if we killed Mr. Centell, it would bring unwanted heat. Being a city councilman would give him even more reason not to go to the cops. I asked Mr. Centell if he had anyone going to our house and he nodded yes. We told him to get on the dock and if the girls were injured, we would hunt him down.

"BH was standing near the wheel of the boat and told me to untie. We headed back to the river. He was worried about the girls. Once we reached the river, we threw the guards overboard and hauled ass toward the house. BH had a suspicion Mr. Centell had sent his people to get the girls for a bargaining tool to get our dope.

"We arrived at the house pier and noticed a van parked near the house. I grabbed the AR-15 and BH picked up a shotgun from down below. I went to the right and BH headed for the front porch. We could hear a man screaming at the girls.

"I looked through the kitchen window and saw through a living room door where two men were standing. One had a pistol and the other had a ball bat. I went back around and found BH. He was at the front window near the main entrance. The girls were sitting on the couch crying.

"I opened the door and slowly walked down the hall. One of the two guys, a black man, was yelling at Rachel, 'Where is the dope? Tell me or I will blow your head off.' I took aim with the rifle and yelled out, 'Right here, you son-of-a-bitch!' I pulled off three loads and hit him in the arm and right side. He fell onto the couch and turned it over. The other one, a white man, took off running toward the front door and then I heard the shotgun go off and saw him bounce backwards from the door onto the hallway floor.

"Rachel came over and took BH's shotgun and shot the man on the floor three more times. What a mess. It took an hour to clean it all up. We put the bodies on a boat and took their van up the road about ten miles and parked it at a truck stop.

"Heading down the river, we pulled into a small cove and fed the bodies to the alligators. BH said we would head out to sea and go to Tampa, Florida since it was a haven for drug dealers and money laundering. We had nearly three million in cash and five kilos of coke.

"When we arrived in Tampa, we contacted Lonny and he hooked us up with some Cuban drug dealers who had contacts with the banks. We stayed on the boat for about three weeks until the Cubans found us a house near the old cigar district. It wasn't fancy but it had a large pool and small guesthouse in the back. The girls were put up in a beauty shop on a corner down in the cigar district.

"The beauty shop would be used for laundering money.

"The Cubans put BH and me in business running one of their car lots. It was also used for laundering money. There was a car lot every hundred yards and all of them financed vehicles. We were really surprised how big the used car business was and how much money they moved in a week. Dope and money were hidden in the cars and they were picked up by other drug dealers and moved from one part of the city to another.

"We moved as many as twenty cars in one day. No one ever knew which cars had the dope or money. They got paid to move them and really didn't care what was in them. The same car would come and go from the lot at least four times a month.

"The amount of drugs and cash shocked even us. All of it was moving right under the noses of cops. The cops would come in and borrow a nice Mercedes to impress their girlfriend, drive it a month, and come back and get another one. The Cuban kingpins had small modest houses around Tampa. They had nice condos on the bay waterfront under the name of girlfriends or a name out of a graveyard.

"The Cubans were very ruthless and it didn't take us long to observe it firsthand. Lonny had told the boss, Ricardo, we could be trusted to do anything. Ricardo's driver picked us up one day at the car lot and told us we needed to collect some cash from another lot. Seems they were about a hundred grand short on the pick up the previous week. In Tampa, with all the pretty weather, most of the lots had outdoor garages with one or two hydraulic car lifts. We found the guy in one, working under a car. He was a Cuban around thirty years old.

"It was broad daylight and I could tell the guy knew why we were there. The place was surrounded by a chain link fence, and the driver told BH to close the gate. The guy had no place to go. The driver said something to him in Spanish and the man motioned for us to follow him to a little shed near the lift.

"Just as we walked inside, the air compressor came on and I pulled out my pistol. The guy reached over and cut it off and started, in broken English, to explain about the money shortage.

"BH came in just as their conversation was heating up. The driver, a short stocky Cuban with a large scar across his face, grabbed the guy and pulled him over to the air compressor. He then cut the compressor back on and held they guy's face down to the turning wheel and belt.

"He pushed the man's face down into the wheel and blood flew all over BH, the driver, and me. What a mess. I could smell the burning flesh and see the guy's skin rotating around on the belt of the machine. The driver told the guy we would be back in one day and he better have the money. BH and I looked at each other and headed back to the car. We knew we were dealing with people just as crazy as us. We would never have left his ass alive though.

"We were told they guy came up with the money and we never saw him again.

"After being in Tampa for a few months, Ricardo said he was going to fly the girls and us down to an island for the weekend. He had a twin-engine plane and a pilot. The girls were excited to meet Ricardo and two of his girlfriends at a small airfield outside of Tampa. His girlfriends were beautiful. They were tall, tanned, and had big boobs. They appeared to be in their late twenties. Our girls were a little jealous but loved the new outfits we had bought them.

"After two hours of flying, we broke through the clouds, and could see a small island. By the time we landed at the small airport, I knew where we were. We were in San Pedro. I could see the bridge over the water near the ocean front. Small boats were lit up along the shore. We were picked up by a white four-wheel drive Ford Explorer. It was odd to see a car among all the golf carts.

"We headed north and pulled up to the bridge, and the same guard that I had given the twenty-dollar bill was still there. The driver gave him a twenty and we moved on. After about ten minutes, the concrete road turned into gravel and we were headed out into what looked like the jungle. The road was rough and the car started to bounce everyone around.

"We reached a large hotel looking structure just off the oceanfront. It looked as though someone had invested a lot of money, but it appeared to be unfinished and no cars were in the huge parking lot. No lights were visible but two men were standing at the main entrance.

"Once we entered the building, it was obvious this place was Ricardo's home or the home of one of his friends. All the windows were covered by black drapes. There was a check-in desk, marble floors, and columns. A large pool was outside and the bay waters could be seen just beyond the pier.

"Rachel and Kee were told to follow Ricardo's girlfriends. We made our way out to the pier and boarded a small fishing boat. Ricardo told us we were going to talk business at a private cabana. It was only about fifteen minutes from the hotel and we had to go down a narrow channel to reach it. It was built in the traditional manner of the Caribbean with a thatched roof and lots of stone. The outside was covered in something that looked like small bamboo. A lily pond lit by small candles surrounded a small fountain in front of the entrance.

"Two young females greeted us with punch and rum drinks. They left the drinks and came back with a box of cigars, pulled them out and licked them in a sexy manner, lit them and placed them in our mouths. We sat around a small firebox and had a few drinks.

"The girls disappeared and the driver returned with a larger wooden box. Ricardo opened it and pulled out a handful of small blue tablets. He said, "Men, this is the next thing; it can get you high in ten seconds and keep you that way for two days. It costs five cents to make and will sell for five dollars each. You can put a thousand of them into a Coke bottle."

"He pulled out a bottle of Coca-Cola, looked at us, and said, 'What is this?' I looked at BH and said, 'It's a bottle of Coca-Cola.' When I picked it up, it appeared to be a bottle of Coke; I could see the cola inside. Ricardo laughed and said, 'No, my friend, watch.' He twisted the bottom of the bottle off and showed us that the liquid was only at the top and the remainder of the bottle was painted on the inside.

"It was a fake bottle. He scooped a handful of tablets from

the box and poured them into the bottle, laughed, and said, 'Self-contained, my friend. We will make millions.'

"The girls returned with drinks and Ricardo handed out pills to everyone. Each of us chased the pills down with rum. In less than a minute, I was high as a kite and the room was spinning around. I looked at BH, and he was walking around with his arms stretched out like a flying pelican above the blue ocean waters of San Pedro. The girls were taking their clothes off and kissing each other. I could hear music playing but I couldn't tell where it was coming from and I couldn't understand the lyrics. I just knew it was music.

"The last thing I remembered was that I had an erection. I woke up in a bed with two girls. It was daylight and I had no idea where I was. I couldn't remember how I had gotten there. I still had an erection that wouldn't go down. I went down the hallway and BH was lying on the floor with a cigar still in his mouth. Ricardo was outside on the deck near the lily pond. He was just staring into the morning sunrise.

"It took several hours for each of us to regain our thoughts. We agreed that those blue pills were like nothing we had ever experienced. This stuff could mess up a lot of people in a short period of time. It had to be a hit with the drug peddlers. It was called 'blue microdot acid,' a form of LSD. We spent the weekend in beautiful San Pedro before returning to Tampa to meet the chemist who would make the pills.

"BH and I were told to go to an old warehouse in the market area of Tampa. The building looked as if it were built in the 20s. Some of the handmade bricks had fallen into the alley where we entered the building. We took a noisy freight elevator to the top floor. The elevator was the kind with a pull-up wire screen door and wooden floor.

"A slim old black man was waiting as we got off the elevator. He walked with us down the hall and knocked on the door. A buzzer went off and the door opened. Standing in a hallway were two large

Cubans, one holding a shotgun and the other standing there with a pistol in his belt. We were handed white smocks and surgical masks and told to put them on. The Cuban with the shotgun motioned us to go on down the hall.

"We turned left at the end of the hallway where another Cuban with an AR-15 was waiting for us. Another buzzer sounded and we were told to go inside.

"We stepped inside and were immediately frisked by the guard. He told us to go through a nearby glass door and wait inside. A few minutes passed, and an old man came in and said he was going to show us around. Several large stainless steel tanks filled the center of the huge room. The tanks were about six feet in diameter and six feet high. On tables near the walls were all kinds of test tubes and gauges. Bunsen burners were going in several different locations.

"There was a large walk-in freezer on the back wall. The old man opened the door and showed us rows and rows of glass containers filled with the blue tablets. He said there were about five million tablets there.

"We left the room and walked across the hall into another large room. Inside there were about ten naked women wearing masks. They were putting the tablets in the fake Coca-Cola bottles. The bottles were put on a conveyer belt and disappeared through an opening in the wall. Through another door, we saw more girls putting the bottles into two blue crates. It was one hell of an operation. I asked the lab man why the girls were naked, and he said that was to prevent them from stealing tablets.

Ralph paused to catch his breath. He continued, "The last room we saw was the money counting room. Five old men who looked like they were in their seventies were sitting in front of automatic money counting machines. The money counters looked up from the machines as soon as they finished a stack. They dropped the stacks of money into a round hole in the floor.

"When BH and I got back to the car, he looked at me and said,

'Holy shit!' We thought we had seen a lot of dope and cash in our life but this was really the big time.

"We were really busy in the dope business for the next few months, and it became somewhat stressful for all of us. The Cubans were having a hard time finding customers but BH figured out the problem real quick. Blue Dots weren't something people with a little age on them could handle.

Chapter Twenty

Rage for Blue Dot Pills

"Remembering the night we took the stuff on the island, BH suggested targeting younger adults…people like lawyers and kids right out of college who thought they would conquer the world. Those people and other young adults would be our best customers. They had the energy and contacts with thousands of possible users. We also knew we were too old to find a good contact who would be trusted enough to help us.

"We were in the pool with the girls, and Kee said she had a new customer at the beauty shop that was interesting. He was a young doctor who recently had opened up his own family doctor practice in Tampa. He came in once a week to get a trim. She also said he liked to smoke weed and had a gambling problem. It sounded as if this doctor might be someone to bring into our operation. We only wanted to use him as a contact. If it worked out, we could get the ball rolling.

"Dr. Gary Wayne was a nice looking young family physician. I could see how the girls thought he would fit well in our business. The girls worked on him for a couple weeks, and we finally met him out at Fort Desoto Park. That was a nice place with white beaches and plenty of isolated parking. We spent a day at the beach feeling him out and finally gave him a few tablets to experiment with.

"In two weeks, he was on board. We gave him two-hundred pills at two dollars apiece. He would sell them for five dollars each. The pills cost the Cubans less than fifteen cents so there was big profit for everyone. In two months' time, the doctor had five more doctors working under him. They were moving ten-thousand pills a month and couldn't keep up with the demand. We needed more runners and sellers.

"The Cubans bought a couple of old Coca-Cola trucks and repainted them with the logos and everything. They would deliver the pills by the case on those trucks. At one point, we had fifty stores selling the fake bottles of Coke right under the noses of the cops. The old west side of Tampa was popping the little blue darlings. The cash was building up and even with the banks in San Pedro washing the money, we had to find a way to hold the cash until we could move it to the island.

"We found some land five miles outside of Tampa. It was seven acres with an old house trailer on it. It was part of an old orange grove that had been abandoned. There were only a few dozen fruit bearing trees left along the road down that ran down to the trailer. The trailer and an old shack couldn't be seen from the highway. At the very back of the land were the backwaters of the river.

"We bought a shipping container from a storage company, rented a backhoe, and buried the container behind the shack. Then we fixed a hidden entrance from the shack to the container. We built shelves in the container and were ready to store the excess money. We never told the girls about the land or the container.

"The business was expanding faster than we wanted. Meanwhile, Ricardo was introducing us to more and more of his associates. We wanted to stay in the background but we were quickly becoming more and more refined. And our girls also were enjoying much different lifestyles. I knew down deep that all of this wouldn't last long. I knew BH would have to return to his killing and raping ways. Neither of us would ever change.

"The girls were trying to convince BH to get a bigger and nicer home down near the bay. I was against it and told them if they did, I would stay at the smaller house. It only took a few months before they all moved down to the bay in a house owned by Ricardo. I suspected Ricardo had his own reasons for wanting the girls nearby.

Chapter Twenty-One

Something Strangely Good Happens

"The cash kept rolling in. The desire for my obsession with violence crept back, and I started searching for victims. Plenty of bars provided a large selection of women but I wanted the right one. I would take them out to the trailer and torture them with pleasures of my liking.

"After about a week of searching, I found a nightclub on the outskirts of Tampa. A lot of Mexicans and Latinos patronized the place but it was operated by a white guy who went by the name of High Ball. As usual, I kept a low profile by sitting in a darkened corner of the large block building which was decorated with all kinds of Mexican paintings. Bullfighters, farmers, and dancing senoritas filled the bar. Like most, it was dark and full of cigarette and marijuana smoke that caused a haze against the walls. It had the appearance of a low fog in a Florida swamp. The ceiling fan's only purpose was to move the smoke around the room so everyone could get high. It was the perfect place.

"As I often did, I took a seat near the ladies' bathroom to get a good view of the girls as they stood in line to relieve themselves. Most of the women were in their late twenties to mid-thirties, but a dozen or so were in their early twenties or even still in their teens.

I could always spot the girls in their late teens. They were just plain silly after a few drinks.

"I took my time and cased the place for about two weeks. I didn't want to be seen inside and have to answer any questions. I started parking the van at the far end of the parking lot. With my night vision I could check out the girls who couldn't hold their water and used the back of the building to take a bathroom break.

"I had turned into a BH...a woman killer.

"I knew that some of the girls squatted behind a large green dumpster because they couldn't get into the busy women's room inside. That was where I would make my move.

"I reached the club around eleven o'clock one night and parked the van near the corner of the parking lot about ten feet away from the dumpster. I cut off the lights and waited for the girls. Several came out in groups, used the bathroom and smoked, then returned to the club.

"Finally, a single girl came out and made her way toward the dumpster. She appeared to be very young and had dark hair down to her waist. She was wearing a floral pattern dress slit up the side. She definitely was Mexican. I could almost see her butt cheeks. She was having trouble walking which was a sign of being stoned. This would be easy prey, I thought.

"I went around the left side of the dumpster. When I reached the corner, she was singing to herself as she squatted over the black asphalt. I eased up behind her with my ether rag and quickly placed it over her mouth and nose. Though she weighed no more than a hundred pounds, she put up a hell of a struggle until the ether took her down.

"I pulled her to the corner of the dumpster but had lay her down when I noticed her high heel shoes had fallen off. I went back and picked up the shoes. As I bent down, I heard voices approaching. I froze in a kneeling position.

"It was a white girl who squatted while lighting a cigarette. She was talking to someone around the corner out of my sight. They talked back and forth until the girl finished her squat. She stood, turned and looked my way, and blew a smoke ring into the air before turning and leaving. I have no idea why she hadn't seen me. I picked up the girl and opened the back door of the van. I placed her onto the floor and bound her feet and mouth with duct tape, then headed to the trailer with a lot of anticipation."

Ralph pulled his lighter from his pocket and handed me another cigar. "Want a shot of Jack, Sheriff? Here, have one." As he poured the drink, I looked at his face and could tell he didn't have any facial expressions. Nothing at all! No twitching of an eyebrow or anything. It was as though his face were made of stone. He had a lot of years on him but his jaw line was chiseled all the way up to his lower ear.

Ralph continued.

"Sheriff, when I found out that BH's daughter had asked you to come down, I told BH you wouldn't show but you proved me wrong,"

I took a drink of the Jack and asked why he had thought I wouldn't show up?

"You see, Sheriff, you are known as one tough son-of-a-bitch and a pretty smart one at that. I figured there was no benefit in your coming."

I sat down the glass of Jack. "I gave my word to his daughter, simple as that. I'm a man of my word; I thought we went over this before," I said.

Ralph took a seat and said, "Yeah, that's what BH said but I just figured you wouldn't show and I asked BH if he wasn't concerned that you might turn us in to the cops if he told you the full story of all the shit we had done."

I took another sip of Jack and asked, "What did BH say?" Ralph chuckled. "Hell, he said no one would believe all of it anyway and he would be dead by the time it would be published."

I leaned toward Ralph. "What about you, Ralph? You won't be dead," I said.

He placed his giant hands on the table. "Yep, I thought about that a lot but I have been with BH a very long time and trust his decision on things. We have been through a lot of stuff together."

I could see we finally understood each other, and I asked Ralph to continue the story about the girl in the back of the van.

Ralph said something strange happened that night. "I pulled out of the parking lot and headed out toward the trailer. On the way I had to go through a small town; there were only about four traffic lights and for the most part, only black folks lived there,"

"It started to rain. I cut my wipers on but I had to stop at the first stoplight. As the wipers went back and forth, I looked into the rear view mirror and could see the girl was starting to wake up. I'd looked up at the light and then back at her. I did this several times while waiting on the light to change.

"On the corner across the street was a small red brick church which appeared to be at least a hundred years old. It was tiny and probably couldn't seat more than fifty people. The light still hadn't changed. The rain increased and the wipers couldn't keep up so I turned them on high.

"The girl was starting to wiggle in the back. Up ahead at the next light, I could see a woman and man standing near a car; they appeared to be having an argument. He was pointing his finger at her and she was yelling back at him.

"Finally, the light changed and I eased off. On the way to the next light, I could see the man hit the woman in the face. She fell to the ground and he kicked her in the head several times. Then he pulled her up by the hair and slapped her several times. She went limp and fell back on the street. He kept kicking her.

"There was a small parking lot straight across from where the man was kicking the woman. I pulled the van into the lot under an awning. The man, who was dressed in a tank top and shorts, pulled her by her hair around to the other side of a car. I have no idea why, but I pulled the van over behind the man's vehicle, an old white Oldsmobile. He had the passenger side door open and was trying to put the woman inside when I reached under my seat and got my hunting knife. I got out and walked straight toward them.

"He dropped her and I could hear her head hit the rocker seal on the car as she went down to the pavement. The street gutter was flowing with water and I could see it rolling over her face. He looked up and said, 'What do you want, jerk?' He was a very large black man. I never said a word and kept walking toward him at a fast step. When I was about three feet from him, he pulled a small caliber pistol from his pocket and raised it toward me. 'Look, fool, this is none of your freaking business!'"

"Without saying a word, I pushed his gun hand aside and thrust my eight-inch knife right into his throat. He fell to the ground and I could see and hear the air and blood escaping from the wound. I grabbed the girl and put her into the back of the van. The Mexican was now awake so I took my knife and slit a small hole in the duct tape so she could get more air. I noticed for the first time the beaten girl was black and her face had been cut in several places.

"As I was about to pull off, I looked in my side mirror and noticed a man headed toward the church steps. He was holding an umbrella in one hand and his other was on a small railing. For some reason, against all my fear about getting caught, I backed the van down to the man at the church.

"I rolled down the window and noticed when the man turned around that he was a priest. He turned and made his way over to the van. 'Yes, may I help you, son?' he said. His face had large wrinkles and he looked very old. A scar ran down his right cheek. He smiled and asked again, 'Can I help you, my son?' It was something about his voice It was soft and polite, and it sent a chill down my spine.

"I took a deep breath and asked him if there was a place in the church where I could take an injured woman I had in my van. "She really needs help," I said. Without hesitation, he said, 'Ok, my son, there is an alley in back. I will cut the light on.' I drove around to the alley where I planned to leave the girl on the pavement and get out of there.

"To my surprise, the old priest had the light on and was waiting for me when I arrived in the alley. I reached in the floor board of the van and found an old hoody jacket. I put on the jacket and then joined the priest at the back of the van. I told him to go back into the church and I would knock on the door when I had the girl. Without question, he turned and headed into the church.

"I picked the girl up and carried her to the door. The rain was washing the blood off her face and I could see she had two huge dimples and pretty, straight teeth. I knocked on the door and the old priest quickly opened it. He walked down a hallway and motioned for me to follow. There was a single small bed in a room with a single window. I laid her down and he reached over and picked up a white water pitcher and poured water into a glass.

"The priest looked up at me. He said, 'God will bless you, my son, you have saved this poor soul's life.'

"I looked down at his him and said, 'Father, I am a very bad person and God could never forgive me for all I have done and I don't expect him to. I must go and I hope you forget me as soon as I go through the door.' I walked out of the room and to the van. I checked on the girl in the back. She had managed to work her way up into a sitting position and was leaning against the side of the van. I reached into my tool box and pulled out a six foot chain and wrapped it around her waist and secured it with two locks, one at the waist, one to the spare tire bracket.

"On the ride out to the trailer, I kept thinking about the priest. He never once seemed too concerned about what had happened. He was only concerned about the girl. How could a man be so kind and caring? For the first time in my life, I believe I actually felt guilty about what had happened. Not for stabbing the no good son-of-a-bitch who had beaten the girl but for the priest. I felt as if I should have told him more. BH would never have risked taking anyone to a church. I knew he would be pissed if I ever told him what had happened.

"As I turned down the road to the trailer, the rain let up and I pulled around to the back of the trailer. For some reason, I reached into the dash compartment and pulled out a ski mask. I never used it for the girls I picked up because I knew most would never live to tell. I put the mask on and opened the door to the van.

"The girl was sitting upright and I could see the terror in her eyes. I grabbed her by the ankles and pulled her to the back door. Her dress pulled up revealing her blue panties. Her legs were long and slender, and one of her breasts was close to falling out of the top of her dress. I took the knife and slowly slid it up her legs until I reached her panties. She tried to slide back but I held one foot and told her not to move.

"She was breathing heavily, and sweat was rolling down her face and dripping from her chin. I pulled the tape off her mouth and she took a deep breath. I put the knife to her neck and told her not to say anything. She kept looking at me with big brown eyes, and I could tell she knew it was hopeless for any escape.

"She whispered, 'Please don't hurt me. I'm pregnant. Please!' I had heard this dozens of time before and it never mattered. This was what turned me on, pleas for help. I reached in and pulled her to me and put my lips about an inch from her face and stuck out my tongue. She slowly leaned forward and began sucking on it.

"I could feel her whole body trembling. I was getting excited. She was now in survival mode. She would do anything to save herself. I knew what was going through her pretty little mind. Things like, 'Why did I ever go to the sleazy club? Why couldn't I wait and go to the bathroom inside?' Her mind was now full of all the wrong things she had done that night and she was trying to convince herself she was going to trade sex for her life.

"The moon was making its way through the clouds. Her face lit up from the moon glow and she looked sexier. I spread her legs apart and pulled her closer to me. Her breathing increased as I pushed her panties down to her ankles. I placed the panties around her neck and began to twist them, cutting off her breathing just enough to make her gasp for air. I let the panties go and pulled her even closer to me. She soiled herself and it ran down the groves in the van floor.

"As the moon got brighter, I could see her face and body better. She was indeed young and beautiful. I looked past her and could see my reflection in the rear view mirror at the front of the van. My eyes were cold and I could see me for the monster I am. Strangely, my face changed into the face of the priest. I took my right hand and wiped the sweat from my eyes and his image was still there. I looked at the girl and back at the mirror several times, but the face of the old man was still there. I hadn't done drugs and knew I was completely sober. I asked myself, 'What the heck is going on?'

"I stepped back from the girl and looked up at the full moon. The sweat was running down my back and face. My skin was hot and I felt sick to my stomach. I looked back at the moon and the priest's face was now on the moon. I walked over to the van and while I was opening the driver's door, I looked into the side mirror and again saw the face of the priest. I went over to the steps at the trailer and lit a cigarette. I had to figure out what was going on. This was some weird shit and I had never in my life experienced anything like this even with all the drugs.

"After smoking the cigarette, I walked back to the van and the girl had slid from the back of the van but the chain was holding her. She was on her feet. I put one hand on her neck and the other one on her breast. It was firm and young. Her nipples were hard and her sweat was running down on my fingers.

"I looked in her eyes and gave her a kiss on the cheek. She froze and I could feel her heart beat run rapid. I again looked back to the rear view mirror and again the face of the priest was looking back at me. I walked around to the front and took my hand and jerked the mirror off the windshield.

"I returned to the girl and found her crying. I looked at her for about five minutes. Finally, I took the duct tape and placed a strip over her mouth, pushed her back into the van and shut the door.

"I drove back to the church. By then it was about two o'clock in the morning. I looked at the old Oldsmobile and could see the black guy lying in the gutter; the car door was still open. I pulled to the back of the church. After knocking several times, I opened the door and carried the girl back to the same room as the one where I had been earlier. The other girl was gone but the blood-stained sheets were still on the bed.

"I placed the Mexican girl onto the bed. As I was leaving, I looked back at her and she was nodding at me as if to say thank you. I left and headed to the bay area to find BH and the girls.

"It was at this point, I knew I was getting weaker and knew that I did have some emotions about another human being. It had to be the priest. I needed some drugs and in about an hour, I was with BH and the girls who were already messed up at the big house on the bay.

"It took me a week to get over the experience I'd had with the priest. Like most murders in the big cities, there was only a small article about a suspected pimp being found dead on the sidewalk. I knew from that point on, I would never be quite the same again. I never did tell BH and the girls about it. They were absorbed in the coke and the blue pills. We had enough money and in my mind, it was time to leave Tampa. Maybe somehow I could get on with somewhat of a normal life. If not, I figured we would all be dead within a year."

"We started taking in more and more cash from Ricardo and within eight months, we had nearly seventeen-million dollars hidden in the buried storage container. All of the shelves were stacked full of ten thousand dollar bundles. The operation had grown to nearly a hundred people moving the cocaine and blue dot acid.

"The young doctor became a problem. He was living high and was drawing too much attention to himself. A family doctor doesn't make the kind of money to purchase a small airplane and a half a million-dollar boat. As in just about all cases with drug dealers, it's the wife or girlfriends who put you into prison, and the doctor was giving both his wife and girlfriend too much information. BH and I knew we had to do something about him. The doctor was warned several times about his extravagance and his loose mouth.

"We knew the doctor's routine and the girls found out that he would be at the dock on a Friday night. Kee and I dropped in on him just as the sun was going down. We had some drinks, and he and Kee did a few lines of cocaine. Although he hadn't planned on it, Kee convinced him to take us on a sunset cruise. I operated the boat while the doctor and Kee partied down on the lower deck. The water was smooth as we left the bay and headed out to sea. We had told Ricardo about our intentions. If we knew anything about anything, we knew how to make people disappear.

"BH and Rachel were going to meet us later in one of Ricardo's boats. The doctor and Kee were really having a good time, and the music was blasting out over the bay. I kept the boat at a legal speed and observed all the buoys and wake zones. After about an hour, I dug out some fishing equipment and cast a line.

"Kee and the doctor were grinding all over each over as the music changed stations. I looked around and Kee was at the console turning the knob on the radio. 'Spanish Harlem' by Aretha Franklin was playing loudly.

"Kee pulled her body close to the young doctor and began to grind on his crotch as the lyrics came out, 'There is a rose in Spanish Harlem, a red rose up in Spanish Harlem.' As the lyrics came, Kee and the doctor moved slowly around the deck. Kee knew exactly what she was doing. She lured the doctor up onto the top deck while I pretended to be fishing. In about ten minutes, she asked me to join them for a drink of tequila.

"By this time, the doctor was wasted and all he had on his mind was to get me wasted on cocaine. That would allow him and Kee to go downstairs to the sleeping quarters. Kee and the doctor did another line of cocaine and soon after, I made my move

"There was a piece of pipe about a foot long inserted into one of the reel holders. Kee moved the doctor over to the railing so they could see the sunset.

"I walked behind him and hit him in the back of the head. He went down to his knees but he wasn't out. I pulled him up and threw him down the stairs to the lower rear deck. Kee and I followed him down and threw him overboard. He struggled for air but quickly disappeared beneath the red seaweed.

"Kee and I had a drink of Tequila and gathered all the glasses and threw them into the ocean. We could see Ricardo's boat approaching about a mile away. We sat there in the fishing chair and watched as the doctor's body slowly made its way out of sight. BH and Rachel pulled alongside the boat and jokingly said, 'What happened. Did the doctor get high and fall off?' Kee looked at him and replied, 'How did you know?'

"It was apparent that with such a large organization now in operation, in-fighting would soon take place. We always kept our thoughts among the four of us. We knew we were involved with people who, as crazy at it seems, made us look like Sunday school kids.

"BH and I talked it over and decided we needed to find a way out. We knew if we just picked up and left, they would eventually find us. We also knew we couldn't kill all of them. Bodyguards surrounded Ricardo twenty-four hours a day. Kee and Rachel might be able to get close enough to do him in but we didn't trust them to be that cool. They were blunt killers and there wasn't anything pretty about their work.

Chapter Twenty-Two

Women Rescued

"We continued to put more cash into the container and had nearly forty-million dollars. According to Ricardo, he had locations with over a hundred million dollars stored.

"The girls flew down to Belize with Ricardo and his people. BH and I took advantage of the situation and started to plot an exit plan. We drove over to Louisiana and met with an old friend. He had a farm of more than two-hundred acres, and we bought it for cash. We buried two containers on the farm. We had the friend purchase an old backhoe that would be used to remove the cow dung from the large barn. The place had about fifty beef cattle and this made a perfect cover. Our plans were to simply retire to the farm and live in peace with the girls.

"When we returned to Tampa on Monday, the girls weren't at the house and we couldn't reach them on the phone. We contacted one of Ricardo's girls and she told us that Kee and Rachel had decided to stay back at San Pedro for a few days. BH got really pissed and called Ricardo but he didn't answer the phone. He made several attempts to contact Ricardo. Finally, BH told me to call the little airport outside of Tampa and make plans for us to fly down to the island. We loaded some weapons and headed down to the airport where a single engine plane was waiting. He gave the guy two-thousand dollars and we made the flight down.

"After landing at the San Pedro airport, we rented a Jeep and headed to the house where we had first tried the blue dot acid. Two guards were at the door and we asked to see Ricardo. They hit him up on the intercom and then advised us to go on in. When we entered the large room, we saw him out by the pool with three girls. By this time, BH was pissed and went right to the point. 'Where are our girls? Are they here? They better be.'

"Ricardo was sipping on red rum and had a cigar in his right hand. He lowered his sunglasses to the bridge of his nose and started to explain. 'We all went over to Caye Caulker last night and got wasted at a friend's house. The girls were too messed up and spent the night. We plan to take the boat over around noon and pick them up.

"BH's face was red as the sun, and I knew all hell would break loose if something had happened to the girls. BH bent down and got right up in Ricardo's face and said, 'Call them. Call them right now.' One of the girls handed Ricardo a phone and he began dialing. He started speaking in Spanish to someone on the phone. After a minute he informed BH the girls were still passed out. I walked over to look at the boat dock and saw Ricardo's boat tied to the dock. I told BH about the boat and he told Ricardo he was taking the boat and that Ricardo or one of his men needed to come along to show us the house at Caye Caulker.

"Ricardo told one of his men to go with us to the island. It was about an hour's ride over to Caye Caulker. When we were about half a mile out from the shore, the driver of the boat pointed to a house on a hill. He spoke in English and said, 'That is it right there, the one with the thatched roof.' I looked at BH and he looked back at me. We were familiar with the house. It was the same one where we'd had the shootout and had taken the dope and money. I turned and looked at the driver and I could tell he was nervous. I asked him if he was at the party last night and he nodded.

"BH walked over to the driver. 'I'm going to ask you one time and one time only. Did you see our girls there last night at the party?' The driver had sweat rolling down his face and said, 'Yes, I saw the women.'

"'Are they ok?' BH asked, as he grabbed the driver by the neck. The driver, trying to keep his hand on the wheel, replied, 'I cannot say. I cannot say.'

"I stepped over and put the barrel of my Colt .45 automatic on his lips. 'You have two seconds to tell us about the girls or I'm going to blow your head off.' The man started to tremble and then I heard a shot and the man fell. BH had shot him in his calf and the man was screaming while blood ran down his leg. BH sat on top of him and yelled, 'Tell us what the deal is or I'm going to shoot the other leg and throw you overboard!'

"BH bent down and placed his pistol on the other leg. 'Talk, you son-of-a-bitch!' The man raised-up and screamed, 'Okay, okay but Ricardo will kill us all, I promise you. It's a trap. Ricardo brought the girls over last night and shot them up with heroine. Then he gave them to Carlos, the brother of the man you shot the night you came to his house on the hill. The last time I saw the girls they were in the guesthouse with three of Carlos's men. They were all naked and passed out. Ricardo was going to have Carlos ambush you today because he knew you had been skimming money from him. He knew you would come after the girls. I am supposed to call Ricardo when it's all over and he will come to the island.'

"BH laughed and looked the driver in the eye. He said, 'You may have just saved your ass my friend.' I got the first aid kit and placed a bandage on the driver's injured leg where the bullet had passed through. I pulled the guy off the floor and put him back in the seat and told him to hold the boat steady. BH put the gun back to his head. 'What's your name, amigo?'

"'They call me, Arturo. It means bear-man.' BH put his pistol under Arturo's chin and said, 'I guess you don't feel much like a bear right now, do you, amigo? How many people are on the island with the girls, Arturo?' BH took a seat on the side of the boat.

"Arturo pulled the throttle back on the boat and replied, 'Four men and the girls. Two men are passed out with the girls in the guesthouse.' BH walked toward the front of the boat and looked at the house on the hill. 'Is there a way to get to the house without being seen?' He continued staring at the house. Arturo told us we would have to go around to the other side of the island and dock there. We could get a golf cart and drive close to the house, then walk in from the rear.

"We tied the boat off at a shabby pier and walked into the little town of Caye Caulker. Arturo and I stayed with the boat while BH walked the short distance to the village and rented a golf cart. Then we headed to the south end of the island. On the way, Arturo pleaded for his life with all kind of deals. He told us he had many contacts to get us back to the United States without going back to the San Pedro airport. I knew what BH was going to do with this poor guy. I just listened to him all the way up the hill.

"Once we reached the peak, Arturo pointed out the guesthouse where the girls were last seen. He also told us that one of the two men would be down at the pier waiting on our boat to arrive. I knew the only thing keeping Arturo alive was that we needed him to answer the phone when Ricardo called.

"We made our way close to the house and I could see one of the men down at the pier. He was carrying an assault rifle and was dressed in a bright yellow shirt and tan shorts. I went over to the window and saw another man sitting beside the pool looking at a magazine. He had a blue bandana around his head. His assault rifle was leaning against a marble column about five feet away. There wasn't a door from the outside to the pool, just a breeze way. The man was in deep thought as I eased up on him. Just as I was about to stick him, he turned around and ran for the assault rifle. I tackled him and we struggled and rolled all over the floor. I was sticking him with the knife as we rolled over. I stuck him at least ten times. He tried to yell and I stuck my knife in his mouth and cut his face from mouth to ear. He tried to make a noise but the blood was filling up his mouth. He began to choke on his blood and I finally made the fatal blow to his throat. I was covered with blood from head to toe.

"I picked up the assault rifle and moved out to BH's location. He was now in a position to keep an eye on the guy at the pier. I moved over to the guesthouse and looked into the window. In the main room, I could see one man on the floor with the rubber hose still on his arm. It looked like he had overdosed and wasn't moving.

"I put the rifle at the ready position and slowly made my way into the house. I went down a long hallway and found the master bedroom on the right. I eased around the corner of the door and spotted the girls in a bed with a black male. I could see the needles on the night stand beside the bed and a bottle of rum on the bed with them. They were all naked and no one was moving.

"I went back into the big room, cut the throat of the guy on the floor and returned to the bedroom. Inside the bedroom, I walked around the bed and stood over the black man lying between Kee and Rachel. He was breathing and covered with sweat. I checked the pulses of Rachel and Kee, and they seemed to be okay. I went into the bathroom and found a washcloth. Then I looked out the window and saw BH was still watching the man on the pier. I returned to the bedroom and took the wet cloth and placed it on the black guy's face. After a few seconds, he started to move.

"I placed the knife on his throat and took my finger and rubbed his nose. He opened his eyes and started to raise his head. I took the blade and slowly pushed in through his skin and stopped about two inches in. He started jerking so I climbed up on the bed and pushed it another two inches deeper. Now he was struggling to breathe and realized what was going on. The girls never moved.

"The blood shot out of his throat and covered me, the bed, and the girls. He tried to get up but I held him down and twisted the knife to inflict even more pain. He bled and I pulled him off the bed and watched as the blood covered the beige tiled floor. I walked back to the entrance of the house where I could see BH several yards away. After getting his attention and giving his a thumbs-up, he motioned me to join him. I told him the situation in the guesthouse. Of course, he showed no emotion. We were waiting on Ricardo. The man on the pier didn't know what had happened in the house.

"Ten minutes passed and BH finally joined me in the bedroom. He walked over and looked down at the girls. He walked around and sat on the edge of the bed near Kee. With his right hand he pulled her long hair away from her face and looked at her. He never said a word.

"I told him that both were overdosed and we needed to find a doctor. I knew as soon as I said it, it wouldn't be impossible to find a doctor. However, Arturo said he knew of someone who handled all the overdoses on the island. The woman, like most of the so-called doctors on the island, wasn't actually a doctor but somewhat like a medicine lady. Translated, this means she is or was, a drug addict herself. We went back up on the hill and watched the man on the pier. He was sitting on a small bench and smoking a cigarette.

"The assault rifle I had taken from the man inside the main house was equipped with a short scope, so I scoped the man at the pier. While I was looking, BH and Arturo walked down to the main house. As I watched them enter the house, I could hear the phone ringing. In about five minutes, BH and Arturo returned. Ricardo was about ten minutes out. He had spoken with Arturo who had told him we were all dead, including the girls. We were concerned about the man on the pier but knew Ricardo would be expecting the man to greet him upon his arrival.

"I knew BH was a better shot than me so I handed him the rifle. In about fifteen minutes, the boat appeared and made its way alongside the pier. The man waiting tied Ricardo's boat which carried two more bodyguards. One of the guards was dressed in a Hawaiian shirt. He got off first and put his hand out to help Ricardo off the boat

"Once all three were off and headed down the walkway, BH

squeezed off the first round. It struck Ricardo right in the middle of the chest and knocked him off his feet. The two bodyguards reached down to help Ricardo and BH put a round in both of them. One fell off the pier into the water. The other one was trying to crawl back to the boat. The guard stationed on the pier starting firing in our direction. BH put a round through his head and I could see the blood and skull fly in the air and splash on the sea.

"We put Arturo out front and walked down to the pier. I pulled out my .45 and put a round in the head of each of the victims. Both men in the water were face down on the shore. I stepped down onto the beach and put a round into their heads and left them for the seagulls. Arturo was getting really nervous but I knew we again needed him to get help for the girls.

"Arturo got on the house phone and in about an hour, an elderly lady and her daughter showed up driving a golf cart. She had a doctor's bag and after about ten minutes, I recognized her. It was the same lady who had patched up Kee the first night we had come to San Pedro. The old lady said it would take a while but we told her we were in a hurry to leave. We decided to take her, her daughter, and Arturo with us. We could not wait on the island. It would be only a short time until Ricardo's men would be showing up.

"We carried Kee and Rachel down to Ricardo's boat and headed out to sea with the whole damn bunch. Arturo knew of an island with a perfect cove where we could spend the night. The old woman worked with Kee and Rachel as they puked all night. By daylight, they didn't look much better. I knew what was on BH's mind. If the girls didn't improve, we would have to kill them too. The old woman, her daughter, Kee, and Rachel would have to die. This had been our style for years; we always eliminated the problem completely.

"We were in a bind and we knew it. By this time Ricardo's men knew what had gone down and our going to the airport was out of the question. We had only one choice...head toward the mainland and Belize City. The marina would be a good place to find a way back to Tampa. We had only around four-thousand dollars cash on us and we didn't own credit cards.

"We headed out around 2:00a.m. and made our way into the marina without any problems. Arturo found a boat crew from Honduras that was willing to take us to the coast of Mexico. BH had contacts there and we could get a boat ride to Tampa. We had to get the girls sober. If the Coast Guard boarded us, the sick girls would surely draw attention to all of us. I was surprised BH didn't kill the old woman and her daughter before we reached the marina, but he was going to give the girls a chance to improve on the ride to Mexico.

"The Hondurans took us all on a small freighter that had a crew of ten. It was headed toward Tampa. We were taken downstairs to a large area near the engine room. Arturo gave the captain the cash and, in Spanish, the captain told him where there was a hiding place located on the back side of the engine room. The place reeked of diesel fuel and the engine noise was deafening to the ears. We all settled in for the voyage to Mexico.

"We arrived at a small fishing village but had to anchor the boat about three hundred yards from shore. The girls were showing signs of improvement. BH and the old woman took the dingy to shore to pick up some medication at a drug store. I told the girls to get with it and try to overcome the sickness. Both of them knew what I was talking about. They wanted to know how pissed BH was, and I simply said, 'You know.'

"BH returned with the medication and had acquired a boat to take us to the Louisiana coast. There he would contact his uncle about getting us a car and some cash to proceed to the new farm. From there we would devise a plan to go back to the buried container near Tampa.

"A crew of three Mexicans was in charge of the charted boat BH had secured. It was an old vessel but it ran smooth and the Mexicans worked cheap and knew all the ends and outs of getting past the Coast Guard. The sea was rough, and that didn't help the recovery of Kee and Rachel. None of us had been near soap and water for almost three days. The stench was blowing through the gulf winds. BH and I had to make a serious decision about the girls

"When we reached the Louisiana Gulf, BH's uncle was waiting with a van and some cash. We loaded the whole crowd and headed to the farm. We noticed the old backhoe had been delivered and electricity was on in the house. The old house had faded white paint and looked to be at least a hundred-years-old. It has a wraparound porch that accented the green printed tin roof. There were two large fireplaces, one at each end of the house.

"Upstairs, each bedroom had a small fireplace and large nine-pane windows. Out back near an old corncrib was a double door outhouse. Several old buildings dotted the overgrown yard which had wonderful shade provided by nearly a dozen big magnolia trees. The most noticeable structure was the giant barn that rested atop a small hill a couple hundred feet from the main house. It had no less than 15,000 square feet of space. There were six stalls on each side of the lower floor and nearly a thousand bales of hay in the loft. The beef cows were down by a three-acre lake that had a pier and water mill pump on the dam side.

"The farm was nearly a mile from the dirt road that came off a state road two miles away and would be easy to defend from intruders. BH's uncle stayed around for a few days to pick up supplies for the house and he tune up the old backhoe. After everyone was settled in, BH and I headed back toward Tampa to see if we could retrieve some of the money.

"We arrived at the old trailer at 2:00a.m. and used a backhoe to open the entrance to the buried shipping container. After a long discussion, we decided to take only five million dollars with us. If stopped, we would have plenty to secure for bonds and lawyers.

"The trip back was uneventful and we stored the money in the barn loft. As the days passed, Rachael' and Kee's conditions improved to the point they were now mobile and eating solid foods. Rachel told me that facing BH was her biggest concern. Two weeks passed and BH never mentioned the girls and the mess with the guy in the bedroom. We all started back drinking and doing coke as though nothing had ever happened.

"One morning after an all-night rainstorm, I looked out through the fog and heard the backhoe start up near the barn. It was still raining and I could barely see the headlights on the old machine. It was headed down to a gulley near the lake. As I dressed, I could hear the engine rev which indicated that BH or Arturo was digging with it.

"I finished dressing and started the long walk down to the lake. The raindrops were running down my face as I put on my rain jacket. BH was seated on the old red and gray tractor operating the controls. He was sitting in front of the controls without a raincoat as though it was a pretty spring day. I walked near the machine as he eased up on the throttle. 'Go back to the house and get Arturo and the old woman and girl,' he said.

"I knew what he meant so I made my way through the mud and slush back to the house. Pulling the pistol out from under my mattress, I thought how those three had helped us make our way back, but I knew it would be futile to try and persuade BH to let them go.

"I went upstairs and got the old woman and girl up and bound their hands. They were in their gowns and shaking while I put the duct tape around their mouths. We came out of their bedroom and Rachel was standing in the hall wearing panties and a t-shirt. She stared at me while shaking her head back and forth to indicate her disapproval. I told her to get Kee and come downstairs. When we got downstairs, I reached under a couch cushion and gave Kee a .357 Magnum pistol and told her to hold the old woman and girl in place.

"Back upstairs, I flipped the light switch and Arturo rolled over and put his hand over his eyes while saying, 'Que ocurre?' He was asking what was happening. I pointed the pistol at him and told him to turn around. Securing his hands behind him with duct tape, I guided him toward the door but he tried to run toward the stairway and I hit him in the back of the head. Once I had him downstairs, we all headed to the lake. Rachel had put on jeans while Kee had found a robe. We all marched through the mud toward the lake.

"BH had finished digging the hole and was standing by the backhoe when we arrived. The old woman and girl were shaking as the rain soaked their hair. Arturo was groggy from the blow to the head and was leaning back and forth. BH, without saying a word and showing no expressions, walked over to Kee, took her pistol, and shot each of them once in the back of the head. Their bodies fell and slid down the slimy bank into the bottom of the pit. BH gave the pistol back to Kee and said, 'Go on back to the house and fix breakfast.'

"The girls left as I stood there watching the three bodies now floating in the rainwater in the bottom of the pit. I could hear the backhoe engine roar as I turned and walked back to the house.

"When I entered the house, Rachel and Kee were in the kitchen preparing breakfast. None of us said a word. We knew not to ever show any emotion about anything when BH was in one of his killing moods. Forty-five minutes later, BH came in. 'I hear there is an old plantation for sale about ten miles from here. I think we should all ride down and take a look at it.'

"We spent the rest of the day in the kitchen drinking and doing cocaine. The girls stayed away from the coke but drank some Jack Daniels. The next morning, BH and I cranked an old sixty-two Chevy truck and drove it around on the farm. Afterwards we took it down to a little service station to get some gas. While there, BH bought a lottery ticket and threw it onto the dash of the old sidestep truck. This was odd because I never had seen BH buy one.

"We never did go down and look at that old plantation. BH kept talking about it but somehow we never found time to go down there. We eventually would move into that place. But that's another story you probably have already heard, Sheriff. You know that is the place where we are now.

"We lived a very quiet life for a while until the girls wanted to go down to New Orleans for a weekend. I knew the thugs down there hadn't forgotten the shooting we'd had near the dock. I voiced my concerns about going back to the Crescent City. Still, BH made the decision to go and we left on a Friday night.

"On the way down, BH started to cough up blood and we took him to a nearby hospital. He gave them a fake ID and was admitted. He told us to go on and enjoy ourselves and said he was going to be okay."

Chapter Twenty-Three

Bikers Make a Big Mistake

"The girls and I went out to a nearby country bar. The place was crowded and the music was blasting. We took a seat in the back and ordered a bottle of Jack. The girls were upset about BH's condition and took it out on the bottle.

"Before long, the girls were wasted and went outside to the van to do a line of coke. I followed them out and went into an alley to take a leak. When I entered the alley, there were several people gathered near the front. I walked by without looking at anybody. When I reached the end of the alley, I faced a wall and started to relieve myself.

"While I was shaking off, I heard a shuffle behind me. I turned around to find three big biker guys standing in front of me. The one in the middle reached over, placed his hand on my right shoulder, and said, 'Dude, we don't want any trouble. We just want your money.' I zipped my fly and told him to back off and move out of my way. As soon as the words were out of my mouth, the one on the right pulled out a pistol and told me to turn around and back up against the wall.

"My pistol was back in the van, but I had my knife in a holster on my ankle. I had learned a long time ago, however, that taking a knife to a gunfight isn't a good idea. A few words were passed. I punched the big guy in the face, and the other two thugs grabbed me and threw me to the ground. A kick in the face stunned me and I tried to get up. All three began kicking me and I knew I had to reach for the knife.

"After a few attempts, I was able to retrieve the blade, and I stabbed the big guy in the calf. He screamed with pain and backed off. Now it was two against one. I knew if I could get to my feet, I could make it a fair fight. I finally got on my feet but blood running from the cut above my right eye blurred my vision.

"As I tried to wipe the blood from my eyes, I was hit on the back of my head with a hard object. I grabbed one of the thugs while going down and bit his ear as we fell to the pavement. I bit so hard a piece of his ear came off in my mouth. My experience from being in many prison fights told me I had shocked two of them. If I could get back on my feet, maybe I could take on the third one. I was in pure survival mode and it wasn't looking good.

"I spit out the piece of ear and grabbed the third thug by the ankles. As he was falling, I hit him in the crotch and heard him yell. 'You son-of-a-bitch, I will kill you!' I got up and kicked him the mouth. His teeth bent backwards and blood rolled down his chin.

"Now that all three were wounded, I decided to get back to the van and get the girls and the pistol. I was half way down the alley when the big biker caught me from behind and hit me in the head with what felt like a pipe. I fell against a retaining wall and started to lose consciousness. My blurred vision allowed me to see only an outline of the big biker standing over me. As I tried to raise my head, I heard someone say, 'Get his wallet and finish him.' I was thinking to myself, 'What a hell of a place to die.

"I lay my head back down and prepared for the end. As soon as my head touched the asphalt, I heard Rachel's voice. 'Back up, you bastards, or I will blow your heads off.' Kee reached down and put her hand behind my neck. 'Get up, Baby. We will take care of these assholes.'

"I got up and wiped my face. I could make out Rachel standing there in her mini-skirt and holding the .357 Magnum in a two-hand combat grip. Rachel walked over to me and said, 'You okay, Baby?' I told her yes.

"Two of the bikers were standing and the one with the missing ear was on the ground holding an old newspaper against his ear. The big thug who had gotten my knife in his leg was staring defiantly at me like nothing had happened. The blood was still trickling down his face.

"Kee walked over to Rachel and took the pistol. 'Give me that. I will show these assholes who they're messing with.' She walked up to the big guy and shot him right in the face, and the back of his skull flew past the biker behind him. One biker turned and ran back into the alley against the wall. As Kee passed the biker on the ground, she put a round in the top of his head. When she reached the third one, he was on his knees saying, 'Hey, you crazy bitch, you don't know who you're messing with.' She answered, 'Oh yes, I do. I'm messing with the punks who messed with my man and now you're going to join them in hell!' She pulled the hammer back and put a round into his crotch and one in his face and walked over to me. 'Come on, Baby, let's go check on BH.'

"We headed back to the hospital to check on BH.

"I stayed in the van while the girls went into the hospital to speak with the doctors. When they returned, the news wasn't good. BH was eaten up with cancer and there weren't any treatments that could save him. All we could do was make him comfortable until it was his time to go. The girls took it really hard.

"The next day we went to BH's room and that's when he told us about having a daughter. He had spent some time with her recently when he had been gone for several days. He'd never told us where he had been. None of us had had any idea he had a daughter because he had never had mentioned her.

"We rented a motel room near the hospital and stayed with BH for three days until BH got strong enough to ride back to the farm. We headed back up the highway with BH lying in the back with his head on Kee's lap. Rachel and I held down the front, and there wasn't much talking as I held the old van steady on the speed limit.

"BH did tell us that he had a surprise for us. He had bought the old plantation before he had fallen sick and had been waiting to surprise us. It was that same old plantation he had told us about earlier...the one he'd wanted us to check out but we'd never gotten over there together to look at it. He paid cash for the place with money from the big lottery ticket his daughter had cashed in for him. I'm sure his daughter told you about that when she contacted you.

Chapter Twenty-Four

One Hell of a Ride

"BH wanted to the plantation as soon as possible but was sorry he wasn't able to help with the move. He hoped to spend his final days at the plantation.

"Two weeks later everything was moved from the farm, and the girls and I loaded BH into the camper van for the ride to the plantation. He was now in a wheelchair. His daughter and her husband met us over there and she was really nice. It was the first time I had seen BH smile in a long time. He was really proud of the place and we all went through it together. Maybe, just maybe, we could finally all live in peace.

"A caretaker was hired to look after the farm. He and his family share in the profits from the cattle sales as well as from any crops they might want to plant. We agreed to pay for maintenance of the machinery.

"We got settled into the plantation and the girls loved it. They especially loved the stage downstairs. They would get on stage and sing as I played the piano in a rag-time beat. BH would have his glass of Jack and clap along with them. Kee pushed him around the lake and sang to him while Rachel and I prepared meals in the enormous kitchen. We dressed in era clothes and pretended we were back in the old plantation days. The girls pretended to be Southern Belles and we acted and talked like old Southern Gentlemen.

"Surprisingly, BH's health improved somewhat once we moved to the place he regarded so fondly. He wasn't able to get rid of the wheelchair, but he survived month after month until we had been in the plantation a year.

"We decided to celebrate the anniversary by having a special dinner. We invited BH's daughter and her husband to the big house. It began to rain early that morning, and we had to move everything in from the lake. We held the dinner in the grand dining room around the beautiful red dining table. The girls were so excited about the event. They were even happier about being clean of drugs for nearly a year.

"I was cleaning the stage room when the girls came in and told me they were heading into town to get some things for the party. They were all smiles and said they would be back in two hours or less. I told them to be careful in the rain. Rachel pulled up her dress and showing her thighs and said, 'Baby, you know we're always careful.' She blew me a kiss and I heard them laughing as they walked out of sight.

"Two hours passed and the girls didn't return and hadn't called. BH was with his nurse in the den and told me to go find them. I knew they weren't at a bar. I headed down the winding two-lane road toward a small strip mall ten miles away. The rain was heavy and the wind was blowing magnolia flowers across the truck windshield as I leaned up on the wheel to improve my view.

"Just as I went over a small hill, I could see flashing lights near the old wooden bridge at Jar's Creek. My breath went away when I spotted the rear end of the camper van sticking out of the creek. A large concrete delivery truck was parked in the middle of the bridge. An emergency crew was standing on the bank, and a diver was near the van. He went into the creek just as I pulled over.

"I stood by the side of the truck and waited for him to surface. It seemed like hours as I waited for the diver to return. The diver surfaced and motioned for a second diver on the shore to join him. They quickly surfaced with the motionless body of Rachel. I got down on one knee as she was pulled to shore. The yellow lights from the wrecker were flashing as they pulled the camper from the creek. I saw Kee's lifeless body slumped over the steering wheel. Her long hair covered the wheel while one of her hands was lying on the dash.

"Rachel survived the crash but the time that her brain was without oxygen caused damage. Now, she is just a beautiful body in a wheel chair. BH had Kee cremated and her ashes are sitting on a shelf in the smoke room. I moved Rachel upstairs where she remains today. I look after her but BH hasn't ever been up to see her since the accident.

"As the days passed, BH had me to go up to his daughter's house and bring her down here. He wanted to talk to her about his confession. I wondered about him making a confession; I knew BH wasn't even close to being religious. BH told her to get in touch with you. Although you were a lawman, he liked you and thought you would be the one person who might understand him...how he had gone bad and all. But, Sheriff, I know he isn't looking for pity. BH only wanted to tell it one last time!"

Ralph paused and his voice dropped. "So, here you are, Sheriff. As you can see, our lives are a mess and we are awful disgusting people. God put us together for some reason. I know we will all meet in hell again but we had each other for a little while. It was one hell of a ride. You are the only person I ever knew BH to respect, and I want to thank you again for coming down.

I reached over and shook Ralph's hand. I thought, "This has been a most interesting trip. I can personally say I haven't met two crazier sons-of-bitches in my life, but for some strange reason, it doesn't bother me."

BH passed away two days later, and I was asked by the daughter to stay for the reading of the will which was held in the cigar room of the big house. Ralph and BH's daughter and her husband were seated on the couch while a man in a black suit and tie was seated behind the desk.

As the lawyer behind the desk shuffled his papers, I heard what sounded like a wheelchair with squeaking wheels approaching. A nurse in a white uniform came around the corner and pushed the chair next to Ralph. In the chair was Rachel! I knew so much about her it was as if we were good friends. Her long hair, now grey, lay on her shoulders. She had a dazed look about her and never spoke. She was still beautiful, and I could only imagine how her personality must have been.

The lawyer began reading the will which designated Ralph as the recipient of the plantation and all of its belongings. The daughter was to receive all of his other assets. BH also provided for Rachel to have lifetime care with all expenses being paid by the estate. Rachel had no idea what was happening around her but she did look out the window and smile as the nurse took her away.

I was getting up to leave when I heard the lawyer speak again. "There is one more benefactor." He reached for another sheet of paper. I looked at Ralph and the daughter; both shrugged their shoulders in a negative manor.

The lawyer read: "To Sheriff Gerald Crawford, I bequeath seven acres of land, a backhoe, and the mobile home located at 2670 Old Grove Road, Holloway, Florida.

I was stunned but told the daughter I appreciated her father's kindness. Then I mused, *"Finally, an act of kindness...*even after all the horrible crimes he committed."

Epilogue

Several months after I left the dying Blueberry Hill and his friends and returned to North Carolina, I received a phone call from BH's daughter. She said Rachel and Ralph had been found dead in the old camper, and it had been ruled a mercy killing and suicide.

No funeral was held. They were cremated and, oddly enough, their ashes were put into the same urn. The jar was placed beside Kee's ashes in the mansion.

The daughter Karen had inherited the plantation, the farm, and other assets from Ralph. She still hadn't decided what she would do with the plantation. She was leaning toward selling everything.

A week later, my brother and I made the trip down to Florida. He was retired and wanted to see the old backhoe I'd inherited. He is the farmer in our family and loves old tractors and farm machinery. We stopped at an old store and got a soft drink and asked the owner if he were familiar with the address. He took a swallow of a Pepsi and said, "Yeah, it's about a mile down the road on the left. It used to be an orange grove, nothing there but an old house trailer and a couple sheds."

While my brother took the left to get into the place, I looked down the sandy road and thought about all the stories I'd heard from BH and Ralph. How many trips did they make down this tree-lined old path with loads of cash and who knows how many bodies?

Were the stories true? Did it really matter? My brother knew nothing except that I had bought an old farm down in Florida.

As soon as we pulled around behind the trailer, he raised his small Coke and poured in his Tom's peanuts. "What in the hell made you buy this place way down here in the middle of nowhere?" he asked.

I laughed and said, "I have no idea, big brother. I have no idea." He got the jumper cables and in a few minutes, he had the old backhoe fired up. Then he stopped, pointed, and said, "Well, at least you got some pretty blueberry bushes over there." I looked in the direction where he was pointing. There on a little knoll behind the trailer were three dozen beautiful fruit-filled blueberry bushes.

I walked over for a closer look at those bushes. I could envision BH, Kee, Ralph, and Rachel walking through them, guns in hand, headed to the next town.

My brother yelled, "Are you day dreaming? Lets' try this backhoe out." I looked at him and pointed to the blueberry patch. "You're right; let's try it out right here on Blueberry Hill."

The End

Made in the USA
Columbia, SC
07 February 2019